Bayard Taylor

Prince Deukalion

Bayard Taylor

Prince Deukalion

ISBN/EAN: 9783337380199

Printed in Europe, USA, Canada, Australia, Japan

Cover: Foto ©Andreas Hilbeck / pixelio.de

More available books at **www.hansebooks.com**

PRINCE DEUKALION.

BY

BAYARD TAYLOR.

BOSTON:
HOUGHTON, OSGOOD AND COMPANY;
Cambridge: The Riverside Press.
1878.

RIVERSIDE, CAMBRIDGE:
STEREOTYPED AND PRINTED BY
H. O. HOUGHTON AND COMPANY.

THE ARGUMENT.

That some fashion of a clew may be attached to a work which the Author hopes will not in any case, be found labyrinthine, he hath been advised by various Friends in whose counsel he putteth trust (the same being Poets), to set forth this Argument. He believes that a very few hints will suffice to make clear his purpose to such as apprehend his primary conception ; and that a moderate furniture of explanation concerning the individual characters of the Drama will be all that any willing reader of Poetry needs. Whosoever turneth to the work from mere instigation of curiosity, or in imitation of others whose tastes are of authority, will surely not be edified.

The central design, or — as it might be said — germinal cause of the Poem is to picture forth the struggle of Man (which term always and inevitably includeth Woman) to reach the highest, justest, happiest, hence most perfect condition of Human Life on this planet. The end of all things being prefigured in their beginnings, the attainment of such condition belongs to Man's original destiny. But Knowledge, Religion, Political Organization, Art, and the manifold assumptions of the Animal Nature, by turns promote or delay the forward movement, make season after season of promise deceitful, and cease not continually to assail the faith of Humanity in much that it possibly may, and rightfully should, possess. Such a struggle, prolonged through a period of more than two thousand years, the Author hath endeavored herein to present, using the device of making Personages stand for Powers and Principles, yet (he earnestly desireth) without losing that distinctness of visage and those quick changes of blood which keep them near to the general heart of Man.

In Act I. the reader will behold the passing away of the Classic Faith, and the emergence of Christianity from its hidden places of abode to the daylight of acceptance. From the mouth of the Shepherd he will hear the voice of the unthinking, obedient multitude : in the Nymphs he shall perceive the beauteous Art and Poetry of the ancient world. Should Prince Deukalion and Pyrrha possess veritable Being for him, they may (in the course of the Drama) peradventure appear as the Ideals of possible Manhood and possible Womanhood, decreed from the first, not yet incarnate, nor permitted to celebrate their high nuptials until both shall be fulfilled in Human Life. Then will the Titan, Prometheus, and the Titaness, Pandora, interpret themselves, and even the bright Goddess, Eos, be no longer mysterious, although not yet fairly beheld of men.

In Act II., which opens a thousand years later, Medusa reigneth. Yet is she no figure of the Faith of her day and world, but only of that Ecclesiastical System which essayed to shape and compel to its service all the forces of Life. In the Youth, who afterwards appeareth as the Poet, and in the Artist, an attentive eye will readily perceive historical Persons; nor can the acceptance or rejection of the Muses, remembering the significance of each thereof, long remain obscure. Only must Epimetheus, the after-thoughted, who receiveth access of vigor in looking backward, and groweth reversely from age to youth, be allowed to keep so much of his secret as he may conceal.

Act III. dealeth with whatever part of this present Century the intelligent reader shall consider most fitting. Gæa, the Earth-Goddess, revives, other-featured than of old; the Nymphs resume a shadowy existence through new forms of Art and Literature; Urania fareth freely among men, putting forth haughtier claims to power; and another Faith, whereof Calchas, High-Priest, represents the inflexible, despotic Theology, hath supplanted Medusa in the Lands of the North. With this much direction, — as it were the silent pointing of a finger, — the courteous reader will surely be content.

In the Fourth and closing Act, the Author adventureth only far enough into the Future to predict the beginning of an Era, of which no simply loving and believing Creature of God can fail to discover the prophecy within his own nature. The Author would not dare to lift the veil sufficiently to disclose the visage of that Era, even were it given to him to behold the same clearly; nor doth he need to offer an interpretation of those things which the reader must divine for himself, if he hath understood and accepted all that foregoes this conclusion. Such a reader will everywhere find, and haply feel, in the Drama, the declaration of Growth, Immortality, God; let him, comforted by whatsoever of the triune light, therefrom proceeding, may rest upon the following pages, not stumble over such matters as are born with the Ages and are doomed to die with the Ages!

CONTENTS.

xii CONTENTS.

ACT IV. — A. D. ——?

PERSONS OF THE DRAMA.

Eos, *Goddess of the Dawn.*

Gæa, *Goddess of the Earth.*

Eros.

Prometheus.

Epimetheus.

Pandora.

Prince Deukalion.

Pyrrha.

Agathon.

Medusa.

Calchas (*High-Priest*).

Buddha.

Spirits of Dawn.

Nymphs.

Voices.

Chorus of Ghosts.

Charon.

Angels.

Spirits.

The Nine Muses.

Urania.

Spirit of the Wind.

Spirit of the Snow.

Spirit of the Stream.

Echoes.

The Youth (*Poet*).

The Artist.

Poet (*Act III.*).

Shepherd (*Man*).

Shepherdess (*Woman*).

Mediæval Chorus.

Mediæval Anti-Chorus.

Chorus of Builders.

Four Messengers.

PRINCE DEUKALION.

ACT I.

SCENE I.

[*A plain, sloping from high mountains towards the sea. At the bases of the mountains lofty vaulted entrances of caverns. A ruined temple, on a rocky height. A Shepherd, asleep in the shadow of a clump of laurels: the flock scattered over the plain.*]

SHEPHERD (*awaking*).

HAVE I outslept the thunder? Has the storm
Broken and rolled away? That leaden weight
Which pressed mine eyelids to reluctant sleep
Falls off : I wake ; yet see not anything
As I beheld it. Yonder hang the clouds,
Huge, weary masses, leaning on the hills ;
But here, where star-wort grew and hyacinth,
And bees were busy at the bells of thyme,
Stare flinty shards ; and mine unsandal'd feet
Bleed as I press them: who hath wrought the change ?
The plain. the sea, the mountains, are the same ;

And there, aloft, Demeter's pillared house, —
What! — roofless, now? Are she and Jove at strife?
And, see! — this altar to the friendly nymphs
Of field and flock, the holy ones who lift
A poor man's prayer so high the Gods may hear, —
Shivered? — Hath thunder, then, a double bolt?
They said some war of Titans was renewed,
But such should not concern us, humble men
Who give our dues of doves and yeanling lambs
And mountain honey. Let the priests in charge,
Who weigh their service with our ignorance,
Resolve the feud! — 't is they are answerable,
Not we; and if impatient Gods make woe,
We should not suffer!

                    Hark! — what strain is that,
Floating about the copses and the slopes
As in old days, when earth and summer sang?
Too sad to come from their invisible tongues
That moved all things to joy; but I will hear.

NYMPHS.

We came when you called us, we linked our dainty being
  With the mystery of beauty, in all things fair and
    brief;
But only he hath seen us, who was happy in the seeing,
  And he hath heard, who listened in the gladness of
    belief.

As a frost that creeps, ere the winds of winter whistle,
And odors die in blossoms that are chilly to the core,
Your doubt hath sent before it the sign of our dismissal;
We pass, ere ye speak it; we go, and come no more!

SHEPHERD.

If blight they threaten, 't is already here;
Yet still, methinks, the sweet and wholesome grass
Will sometime spring, and softer rains wash white
My wethers' fleeces.   We, Earth's pensioners,
Expect less bounty when her store is scant;
But while her life, though changed from what it was,
Feeds on the sunshine, we shall also live.

VOICES (*from underground*).

We won, through martyrdom, the power to aid;
We met the anguish and were not afraid;
   Like One, we bore for you the penal pain.
Behold, your life is but a culprit's chance
To rise, renewed, from out its closing trance;
   And, save its loss, there is not any gain!

SHEPHERD.

What tongues austere are these, that offer help
Of loving lives? — that promise final good,
Greater than gave the Gods, so theirs be lost?
Sad is their message, yet its sense allures,
And large the promise, though it leaves us bare.

I would I knew the secret; but, instead,
I shudder with a strange, voluptuous awe,
As when the Pythia spake: 't is doom disguised, —
Choice offered us when term of choice is past,
And we, obedient unto them that choose,
Are made amenable!   Hark, — once again!

NYMPHS.

Our service hath ceased for you, Shepherds!
    We fade from your days and your dreams,
With the grace that was lithe as a leopard's,
    The joy that was swift as a stream's!
To the musical reeds, and the grasses;
    To the forest, the copse, and the dell;
To the mist, and the rainbow that passes;
    The vine, and the goblet, — farewell!
Go, drink from the fountains that flow not! —
    Our songs and our whispers are dumb:
But the thing ye are doing ye know not,
    Nor dream of the thing that shall come!

VOICES.

Flame hath not melted, nor did earthquake rend
The dungeons where we waited for The End,
    Which coming not, we issue forth to power.
We quench vain joy with shadows of the grave;
We smite your lovely wantonness, to save;
    We hang Eternity on Life's weak hour!

NYMPHS.

We wait in the breezes,
We hide in the vapors,
And linger in echoes,
Awaiting recall.

VOICES.

The word is spoken, let the judgment fall!

NYMPHS.

The heart of the lover,
The strings of the psalter,
The shapes in the marble
Our passing deplore:

VOICES.

Truth comes, and vanity shall be no more!

NYMPHS.

Not wholly we vanish;
The souls of the children,
The faith of the poets
Shall seek us, and find.

VOICES.

Dead are the things the world has left behind.

NYMPHS.

Lost beauty shall haunt you
With tender remorses;
And out of its exile
    The passion return!

VOICES.

The flamé shall purify, the fire shall burn!

NYMPHS.

Lift from the rivers
Your silver sandals,
From mists of the mountains
Your floating veils! —
From musky vineyard,
And copse of laurel,
The ears that listened
For lovers' tales!
Let olives ripen
And die, untended;
Leave oak and poplar,
And homeless pine!
Take shell and trumpet
From swell of surges,
And feet that glisten
From restful brine!
As the bee when twilight

Has closed the bell, —
As love from the bosom
When doubts compel,
We go: farewell!

SHEPHERD.

The strains dissolve into the hollow air,
Yet something stays, — a sense of distant woe,
As now, this hour, while the green lizards glide
Across the sun-warmed stones, and yonder bird
Prinks with deliberate bill his ruffled plumes,
Far off, in other lands, an earthquake heaved
The high-towered cities, and a darkness fell
From twisted clouds that ruin as they pass.
But, lo! — who rises yonder? — as from sleep
Rising, slow movements of a sluggish grace,
That speak her gentle, though a Titaness,
And strong, though troubled is her breadth of brow,
And eyes of strange, divine obscurity.
She sees me not: I am too mean for sight
Of such a goddess; yet, methinks, the milk
Of those large breasts might feed me into that
Which once I dreamed I should be, — lord, not slave!

SCENE II.

[*The Same.*]

GÆA.

I travail for my children. Babe, or youth,
Or man attempered unto utmost life,
The mother's care still follows, grows no less.
The swift impending change scarce other is
Than what my sons have borne erewhile, and thriven.
As the thin blood of boyhood, while it takes
The ripening power of increase in its turn,
Distrusts itself, half fears its own rich force,
So, now, it may be.
                    Yet — I change with Man,
Mother not more than partner of his fate.
Ere he was born I dreamed that he might be,
And through long ages of imperfect life
Waited for him. Then, vexed with monstrous shapes
That spawned and wallowed in primeval ooze,
I lay supine and slept, or seemed to sleep;
And dreamed, or waking felt as in a dream
Some touch of hands, some soft, delivering help, —
And he was there! His faint new voice I heard;
His eye that met the sun, his upright tread,
Thenceforth were mine! And with him came the palm,
The oak, the rose, the swan, the nightingale:

The barren bough hung apples to the sun:
Dry stalks made harvest: breezes in the woods
Then first found music, and the turbid sea
First rolled a crystal breaker to the shore.
His foot was on the mountains, and the wave
Upheld him: over all things huge and coarse
There came the breathing of a regal sway,
Which bent them into beauty. Order new
Followed the march of new necessity,
And what was useless, or unclaimed before,
Took value from the seizure of his hands.

Ah me, in those old days how near and fond
Was he, how frank in passion or in fear
His thoughtless adolescence! To my life
The birth-cord still unsevered held his own:
He took my comforts, seeking none beyond,
And crept for shelter to my shielding arms.
But now — mistrust, and shame of aid outgrown,
And bitter enmity that springs from shame,
And faith perverse in opposite of faith,
Have made him froward. I am forced to seem
She-wolf or pantheress, a savage dam,
And lose the eager mouth that sought my dugs,
Until its native thirst return: but he, —
Sleep-walking in the senses once so keen,
With eyes uplifted to some distant crown,
That, while it burns, makes other glory dust, —

How long shall he thus wander?—and how bear
The lack of all-sustaining loveliness?
Shall fairest sights and sweetest sounds be dim,
And out of movement die the rhythm of joy,
And beauteous passion lose its power to warm?—
All freedom, exultation, and delight
That lifted him, all energies and high desires
That bore him forth as blow the fourfold winds,
Be lashed and goaded on a single path,
One iron chariot draw?

                Lo! here, the Rose;
The woman-flower he could not choose but love,
Shall he forget it? Shall he turn from breath
Distilled of bliss and bountiful bright hours,
To taste the incense rank in censers burned,
Which seems to mask some odor of decay?

     [*A bud on the rose-tree bursts open:* EROS *appears.*]

EROS.

Not yet am I barred in Hades,
   Though a word unknown hath hurled
The Olympian lords and ladies
   To wail in the nether world!
Let Proteus shift in ocean
   From shape to shape that eludes:
I am one, as the heart's devotion,
   Yet many, as lovers' moods!

GÆA.

Blithe, tricksome spirit! Art thou left alone,
Of Gods and all their intermediate kin
The sweet survivor? Yet a single seed,
When soil and seasons lend their alchemy,
May clothe a barren continent in green.

EROS.

Was I born, that I should die?
Stars that fringe the outer sky
Know me: yonder sun were dim,
Save my torch enkindled him.
Then, when first the primal pair
Found me in the twilight air,
I was older than thy day,
Yet to them as young as they.
All decrees of Fate I spurn;
Banishment is my return;
Hate and Force purvey for me,
Death is shining victory!

GÆA.

Thou art the same, — child of the highest Gods,
Whatever shape they wear, and child of mine!
Reclaim thy heritage! — I give to thee
Maytime, and music, and all odorous herbs,
The whispers of the woodlands and the waves

The dewy lustre of acquainted eyes,
The thrill of meeting hands, and ah! at last
Of lips that cannot hold themselves apart,
Save life, as beauty, perish! Take all these,
And whatsoever else may minister
To sweet, insidious influences and arts
Which are thy being, — ply the treachery
That into blessing soon forgives itself;
Print thy soft iris on white wings of prayer;
Strike dangerous delight through sacrifice;
And interpenetrate the sterner faith
With finest essence of the thing it spurns!

EROS.

With the blind desires and motions
    The innocent child that guide;
With girlhood's shy avoidance
    And boyhood's bashful pride;
With the arts that are simplest nature,
    And the nature that hides in art,
When the voice and the cheeks bear witness,
    And the eye confesses the heart;
With the fond mistrust, and the frenzy,
    That falters, or sweeps above,
When the key to delight in beauty
    Is held by the hands of love;
With the lore of the world's renewal
    In seed or in guarded bud;

With the plunge of the sportive dolphin,
  And the heat of the panther's blood, —
The spells of my sway are woven,
  The flame of my being fed,
And I breathe in a bright existence,
  Though the eldest Gods are dead!
For Love, in the ashes of Empire
  And the dust of Faith, is born;
And the rose of a kiss shall blossom,
  When blight has withered the corn!
                    [EROS *disappears.*

GÆA.

Needless to give! — 't is he already owns.
Before the uncounted cycles of the Past
He was, or I — even I — had caught no life
From the wide-floating elements! Go, then,
Thou beautiful, bright secret of all suns,
All planets, and all unimaginable forms
Upon them sown! Death and decay are things
That dissipate beneath thy radiant eye:
So thou but live, all else shall come with thee,
Now lost, or unto man's indifference
So seeming; yet it hides in wilful sport,
And million-voicèd laughter of the waves
And winds, and million wandering smiles of sun
Forever shall betray it, and assure
Thy coming triumph! I am calm at heart,
Now that I know thou livest: was I mad,
To fear, one moment, thou couldst ever die?

SCENE III.

[*A valley, at the base of the mountains. On the left the entrance to a cavern.*]

PRINCE DEUKALION.

Where art thou, Pyrrha?

PYRRHA (*coming forward*).

Dost thou call, at last?
Awaiting the awakening of thy thought,
Mine own went wandering.

PRINCE DEUKALION.

Whither?

PYRRHA.

Nay, why ask?
What other moods have heretofore been ours
Than hope by doubt o'ershadowed, or else doubt
Made bearable by transient gleams of hope?
But now —

PRINCE DEUKALION.

Now, courage! — such as that we felt,
When they who made us and forefixed our fate,
The Titans, fell! We saw the thunder-blows
Given and taken, saw the ruined world
Lie panting after fiercest throes endured,
Till milder Gods brought knowledge, peace, and power.

If, grown familiar, these have forfeited
Their ancient honor, or their term is past,
We need not question ; they consent to see
Themselves in sacred marble rebaptized,
New meanings, borrowed from an alien race,
Bestowed on their Olympian emblems, — yea,
The incense burned to beauty, grace and joy
Made dark and heavy by atoning pain
And crowned repentance! Yet, His law is good
Who now shall rule ; for they we lose withheld
The strength of human hands from human throats,
Forced them to join, and overcome, and build, —
Create, where they destroyed; but He compels
That strength to help, and makes it slave of Love.
Thus, from the apathy of faith outworn
Rises a haughty life, that soon shall spurn
The mould it grew from. I foresee new strife,
Mistaken hopes, unnecessary pangs,
And yet — I wait.

PYRRHA.

And I must wait with thee.
Dost thou recall — how long ago it seems ! —
Mine ancient glory? Nearest, then, I stood:
Our hands — ah, why not also lips ? — had met,
And o'er thy head I saw the hovering crown
Take substance from the air, and flash on me
A glow I hoped was beauty, knew was love!

PRINCE DEUKALION.

'T was when that ether, where the Ages still
Unwrinkled sit, touched by no dread of time,
Was ours to breathe, earth's only sky serene.
Why were we banished? Still that heritage
Exists: beyond the dark-blue, dimpled sea
Lie sands and palms, the Nile's wide wealth of corn,
And soaring pylons, granite roofs upheld
By old Osirid columns: there the sun
Sheds broader peace in all his aged beams,
And hoary splendor on uncrumbled stone.
There still the star Canopus sends the dew,
Though sound of sistrum in the dusky halls
Has ceased, and Memnon lost his morning song.
Well thou rememberest, Pyrrha! — that which was,
Once in the Past, flies forward, like a string
Sharp struck, and straightway in the Future plants
Its brighter phantasm: more than was, shall be!

PYRRHA.

My heart is lifted, and my spirit feeds
Upon thy words.

PRINCE DEUKALION.

                    Pure, patient, brave, thou art;
But they who set thee back, despoiled thy head
Of separate honor, and postponed my right

Through thine refused, were their progenitors
Whose kingdom cometh. Thee they may restore
To equal freedom to renounce and bear, —
Like martyrdom : lend me thy finer sense
To see beyond!

PYRRHA.

So much the Titans gave!
Yet that, reclaimed, is one fulfilment more.
Pain is to me what conflict is to thee, —
A joy, when born of large necessity.
What musest thou? I see thine eyes' clear light
Recede within their depths, as in a lake
Its surface-azure when the cloud sails o'er.

PRINCE DEUKALION.

Erelong some spasm of the vexèd Earth shall close
This cavern's mouth, the last, sole entrance left
To Hades: I would once more see the face
And hear the counsel of my Titan sire,
Prometheus, where he sits in sunless air,
Not suffering, haply, neither glad. And thou,
Heiress of gifts interpreted as woe,
Since the divinest fate wears evil face
To mortals, let thy steps companion mine!
Terrors shalt thou behold, and threatening forms,
And with the stress of stern eternal words
Thy brain may falter: canst thou hear the doom
Which sifts the ages as the fingers sand,

And plays with hope, and patience, and despair,
Like beads upon a string, — inexorable,
Fixed from the first?

PYRRHA.

So I be near to thee.

PRINCE DEUKALION.

Touch, then, my hand! It is permitted us
To feel each other's blood, but nothing more,
Till that far day when our betrothal-kiss
Asserts the victory sure, the empire won!

[*They pass into the cavern.*

SCENE IV.

[*A spacious, arched cavern, opening upon a shadowy, colorless landscape.
Enter* PRINCE DEUKALION, *leading* PYRRHA.]

CHORUS OF GHOSTS.

Away!
Ashes that once were fires,
Darkness that once was day,
Dead passions, dead desires,
    Alone can enter here!
In rest there is no strife,
And memory is not life:
    We neither hope nor fear.

Like some forgotten star,
What first we were, we are.
The Past is adamant :
The Future will not grant
That, which in all its range
We pray for — Change !

PRINCE DEUKALION.

You found the thing you sought : what fashioned else
These sunless realms ? If change may verily come
Even to spirits, teach your dim desire
A form whereby to know itself, and seek !

CHORUS OF GHOSTS.

Retreat ! Retreat,
Unwelcome feet !
Whom doth not blast
The horror of his Past,
Who dares to see
Himself in memory,
And thus reclaim
The inevitable shame,
Him only suffer we !

PRINCE DEUKALION.

Prepare your test !

PYRRHA.

What thing is here designed?
Thy face is pale, despite the firm-set lips,
And level glance of thine unshrinking eyes :
No passing ·pain awaits thee.

PRINCE DEUKALION.

Nay, but power
That grows from pain ! Hear'st thou the whistling rush
Of many wings that part the heavy air,
And bat-like cries, thin, impotent of sound,
That now betray the disconcerted ghosts
Huddling before us to the river-bank ?

PYRRHA.

If I behold these things I seem to see,
I know not : yonder lies a dreary marsh,
Such as at ebb for many a league deforms
A river's narrowing mouth; gray sedges wave,
Unwhispering ever, o'er the slimy flats,
Beyond which glooms the semblance of a shore.
But who is this, so haggard, limp and old,
Approaching us ? As with uncertain joints
He walks, still held erect by senile wrath,
That shoots dull gleams from sleep-desiring eyes,
Were sleep permitted here.

PRINCE. DEUKALION.

'T is surely he,
The ancient ferryman of Hades !

CHARON.

Ay,
Nor vanquished yet! Where wait the ghosts of men?
Hath Death been dispossessed? The upper world
With tears and due libations feeds no more
My sullen river: muddy shallows grow
From either side, and trespass on my right,
Till soon dishonest ghosts may wade across.
Yet, wherefore do I question? You, I guess,
Intend no answer, and eternal Fate
Hath left for you one power of entrance still.
You seek not Lethe: so much say your eyes.
Here lies the other pool, as charged with light
As that with darkness, — awful Memory,
More dread to bear than black Forgetfulness:
Look, or go hence !

PRINCE DEUKALION.

I look.

PYRRHA.

And I with thee.

PRINCE DEUKALION.

Forbear! The knowledge must be mine alone.—
Within the moveless crystal depths, far down,
The rings of ages widen and dissolve
The while I gaze: distinct, abominable,
I see ourselves, before the Titans were;
I see the bestial base, unpurified,
Its hideous features smeared with filth and blood,
Its rites unspoken, acts unspeakable,
Wild savage instinct beating back the brain,
Low savage greed a despot in the heart,
And all that ever since mixed foul alloy
With the bright metal of our dreams, — despair
Should the defiant God within us fail —

[*He pauses.*

PYRRHA.

Say on, nor spare my service! Shall I see,
Thus, only, in the mirror of thy speech,
The unfeatured truth?

PRINCE DEUKALION (*to Charon*).

Is there aught more than this?

CHARON.

Look!

PRINCE DEUKALION.

Nay! — the forms grow dim; and under all
There shines a face that is, methinks, mine own!

[Lifting his head.

What flimsy pride was pierced so, heretofore ?
There is no shame save what begets itself
On old remorse, that keeps its cause alive.
I see, nor shudder: vice outlived is dead,
And feeds its purest opposite in us.
No scent of mould is on the rose's leaves ;
No stain of slime degrades the lotus-cup !
Slave of the Gods, thy lease's term still holds :
Perform thy duty!

CHARON.

· Take the oars yourselves,
And, to your sorrow, cross ! My purse is lean,
So rarely comes an obolus: the boat
Leaks, the worn handles of the ancient blades
Rattle between the thole-pins. Could I push
The beggar ghosts off, crowd my bark with rich,
Enjoy authority, take delight in force,
My limbs were suppler; but ·some power grows slack
In the world's order. One gets old and lame,
And then the Gods themselves forget their words.
Do as you list: nor hinder I, nor help.

[PRINCE DEUKALION and PYRRHA enter the boat.

CHORUS OF GHOSTS.

They go!
Cleaving alone the stagnant flow
Of our deserted river:
Who thus defies the menace and the test?
Is he some hero whom the Gods invest
With warrant to deliver?
Though his disdain
Sharpens our slow, devouring pain,
There wakes an echo in his word
Of what in faded æons once we heard,
That change may come again!
We wait:
Uncertainty at last may bend
Divine decrees, and end
Our fixed monotony of fate!

———·———

SCENE V.

[The Elysian Fields.]

PYRRHA.

Here can I breathe: the sight of cloudy groves
And meadows of familiar asphodel;
The broader lift of this gray vault o'erhead,
Half-luminous, as pregnant with a sun;

The atmosphere of grand extinguished aims,
Suspended hopes or foiled ambitions, — give
Cheer to my soul; for thus in death survives
Something that will not die.

PRINCE DEUKALION.

Why, death 's a thing
For who deserve it! — We defy, and live.

PYRRHA.

What shapes are these, that, as we walk, float on
Beside us?

PRINCE DEUKALION.

Sovereign souls, immortal lives,
That, as a spring through myriad secret veins
Collects the dew and rain-fall, in themselves
Unite all scattered longings of the race,
All formless hope and high necessity,
Distilled through earth to be divinely clear
And flow forever! As in them we live,
So they in us: he, with the bended brow
And parted waves of his luxuriant hair,
Shall yield his shadowy forehead to the thorn
And take a holier name: he, further off,
Within whose dim, dark eyes lie dreams of truth
He never reached, aspires in later souls;
And yonder king who love and lordship gave
To find Humanity, and grew a God,

Now first is regal. These are not the ghosts
Whom irreversible fiat fetters here:
They range the universe.

PYRRHA.

Can they give help?

PRINCE DEUKALION.

Yea! Faith in glorious possibilities
At last secures them.

PYRRHA.

See!—our path ascends,
And near us, pedestal'd above the meads,
Towers a rocky platform, wide and vast,
Where dim Titanic forms, grouped statue-wise,
Express so much of old expectancy
As saves them from despair.

PRINCE DEUKALION.

I see those shapes,
And out of long oblivion memory breaks
To tell me who they are. Pass we the first,
Whose haggard brows and ignorant dull eyes
No promise hold: but yonder, on the rise,
Who leans with folded arms against the stone?
Whose forehead, trenched with subjugated pain,
Still keeps the whiteness of a rising star?

Whose lips, that lock the wisdom of the world,
Have sweetness left for love? Whose huge bare limbs
Affright not, as their force were sheathed in guile,
But rest, in absence of the helping deed?

PYRRHA.

Is he thy sire?

PRINCE DEUKALION.

Prometheus, Titan still!
Seem not reliant, — loose thy clinging hand,
And call the proudest blood that woman owns
To prop thine equal claim!

PROMETHEUS (*rising*).

Come ye with prayers,
Depart!

PRINCE DEUKALION.

Nay, neither suppliant nor subdued!
If no celestial ichor in thy veins
Throbs warm as blood, — no instinct in thy heart
Recalls the primal purpose, and renews, —
No will rekindles, not to war with fate,
But be, thyself, the delegate of fate, —
Then are we not thy children!

PROMETHEUS.

Ye are mine.
I know ye now: will may defiance seem,

Confronted with the force that would destroy.
Thence was I punished; but I set in Man
Immortal seeds of pure activities,
By mine atonement freed, to burst and bloom
In distant, proud fulfilment. When that day
Has dawned on earth, I need no messenger:
My pilfered strength shall of itself return,
And all I purposed be, ere I command.

PRINCE DEUKALION.

I came to question, but thy ready words
Have almost answered.

PROMETHEUS.

Ask, and I will speak!

PRINCE DEUKALION.

Fore-knowledge, eager to fulfil itself,
And too impatient of reverse that foiled,
Provoked thy torture: how shall speech of mine
Shadow the grandeur of thine early aim,
Living in us? Thou knowest, without my words.
But change like this, that now hath fallen on earth,
Came never: never such consoling love
Made overthrow, such promise with one hand
Gave royally, the other taking back.
These things confuse my mind; but all, to thee, —
Both this and what hereafter comes, — is known.

Say, only, shall thy meditated plans,
As in my soul they stir, and hold me up
O'er all discouragement of time and change,
Prevail at last?

PROMETHEUS.

If what I planned could fail,
Were I thy sire? He who defied the Gods
Dares Time and Change, and all reverse of Fate.
I willed what I foresaw: because I willed,
What I foresaw shall be!

PRINCE DEUKALION.

I seek no more.

PROMETHEUS.

But will excludes not love. Since thou, adrift,
And that immortal woman by thy side,
Floated above submerged barbarity
To anchor, weary, on the cloven mount,
Thou wast my representative. My work
Is wrought in thee; thy mother's deed, in her,
Shall yet be justified. Beyond what hope
Comes to thy blood through sense of kin with mine,
Take one new comfort — Epimetheus lives!
Though here, beneath the shadow of the crags,
He seems to slumber, head on nerveless knees,
His life increases; oldest at his birth,
The ages heaped behind him shake the snow

From hoary locks, and slowly give him youth.
'T is he shall be thy helper: Brother, rise!

EPIMETHEUS (*coming forward*).

I did not sleep; I mused. Ha! comest thou,
Deukalion? Once I thought thee strange, distraught,
But now — so many things have happened since —
I think I know thee.

PROMETHEUS.

Soon *thy* work shall come!
Reversely miscreated, forward mind
In thee made backward-looking, shame shall cease
When midway on their paths our mighty schemes
Meet, and complete each other! Yet, my son,
Deukalion, — yet one other guide I give,
Eos!

PRINCE DEUKALION.

Eos?

PYRRHA.

Eos?

PROMETHEUS.

What echoes these?
Who else than she, the genitrix of light,
The mother of the morning?

EPIMETHEUS.

Half I know.

PRINCE DEUKALION.

Older than thou, the stealer of the fire !
More hope in thy mysterious message lies
Than certain-featured forms of prophecy.
But where, when, how, shall I approach her sky,
And win her favoring face ?

PRÒMETHEUS.

Come ye with me !

———·———

SCENE VI.

[*The highest verge of the rocky table-land of Hades, looking eastward.*]

PROMETHEUS.

O Goddess of the far, flushed fields of Heaven,
Swiftly enthroned between the moon and sun,
And swiftly passing as thy roses die,
To make us love thee more ; the dewy-eyed
And blossom-sandal'd opener of eyes ;
Quickener of human hearts, yea, hearts of Gods,
Not one so stubborn but thy smile subdues
To tenderness ; in whom all light and love
Are one, at whose pure lamp all rising Hours
Of hope and deed and victory snatch fire
For torches soon extinguished else, — appear !

EPIMETHEUS.

Deceived so many times, why should she dip
Her shining robes in this unfriendly gloom, —
Why smirch the star that on her forehead burns
And breathe these vapors, when the brighter earth
Forgets her?

PYRRHA.

Speak not thus! What virtue lies
More in achievement than its hot desire?
To shake the drowsed indifference of men
Even Gods are powerless: thy wisdom wears
Sad colors of experience; dark thou showest
Against the light whereto we set our brows. —
But *thou*, who waitest near, as one too proud
Or to evade or spurn shame undeserved, —
Unhappy wert thou woman, angry if
A goddess, tranquil being neither, — speak!

PANDORA.

No other words had opened patient lips.
I have not made complaint, though every sin
Still cheats its base possessor to transfer
Its blame to me, — though she, who now my place
Usurps, takes Egypt's serpent for the Gods,
And eats the apple, not on Ida's hill!
The passion of the race offends its pride,
So this turns back on that, and finds its source —
Where, but in us? Wilt thou accept it?

PYRRHA.

No!

PANDORA.

There is no sign in yonder moveless mist
That she hath heard: thine answer bids me call. —
O Goddess, that from sleep and guilty dreams
Sprung from the dregs of day, from weary vice
And all suspended selfishness of men,
Bidst one pure moment breathe upon the world,
Renewing youth and beauty ere the sun
Shall lighten wrinkles and thin hair, — whose heart
Dreams back Tithonus and dear early love,
And morning visions of unwedded girls,
And sweet desires of uncorrupted men,
Shy as thou art, because divinely proud,
Proud as thou art, because divinely pure,
Hear thou my woman's voice!

PROMETHEUS.

Thine hath she heard.
Faint, rosy gleams, unused to Hades, steal
Forth from the sullen vapor: here no star
May rise before her, nor the clover-dews
Refresh her feet; but every nightly crag
And jutting foreland of invisible hills
Is angered with the glory!

PANDORA.

Goddess, rise !
Forgive the darkness, not of us : so much
As we may see, so much may hear, reveal!

[A sound, as of trumpets.

EOS (*unseen*).

So far away
From my high vestibule of Day,
What voices call ?

PROMETHEUS.

Titan and human, each and all.

EOS.

I, long withdrawn,
Leave to my Hours the service of the Dawn :
The Earth, henceforth, shall see
Only their lower ministry.
But when the race
Lifts unto me a fixed, believing face,
I will return !

PRINCE DEUKALION.

Say, shall not I that distant glory earn ?

EOS.

Thou ! — thou and she,
Inheritors of holy destiny !
　Faith, when none believe ;
　Truth, when all deceive ;
　Freedom, when force restrains ;
　Courage to sunder chains ;
　Pride, when good is shame ;
　Love, when love is blame, —
These shall call me in stars and flame !
　Thus if your souls have wrought,
Ere ye approach me, I shine unsought !

PROMETHEUS.

Yea, under thee the wavering tide
Of the Ages that, stream-like, wind as they glide,
　Shall mirror or lose the gleam,
And brighten as truth or darken as dream !

EOS.

If he but guard his youth,
His dream shall be wondrous truth !

PRINCE DEUKALION.

Call, command ! — I obey :
When there is Dawn, there shall be Day !
4

PYRRHA.

I feel, I love, I see! —
Faithful to him is faith in thee.

EOS.

Oft shall I lift the dark
With fringe of brightness and starry spark;
Oft shall I seem to rise
With the glory of Gods in the waiting skies;
But the Hour shall miss its place,
And the shadow recede on the dial's face!
Say, are ye strong
To endure the wrong
That cheats the promise and mocks the trust?

PRINCE DEUKALION.

I have borne, and shall bear, — because I must.

PYRRHA.

The end shall crown us: The Gods are just.

EOS.

When darkness falls,
And what may come is hard to see;
When solid adamant walls
Seem built against the Future that should be;

When Faith looks backward, Hope dies, Life appals,
Think most of Morning, and of me!

[*The rosy glow in the sky fades away.*

PROMETHEUS (*to Prince Deukalion*).
Go back to Earth, and wait!

PANDORA (*to Pyrrha*).
Go: and fulfil our fate!

ACT II.

SCENE I.

[A wayside shrine, opposite a fountain. Fragments of antique sculpture — among others the head of a Muse — appear in the wall of a vineyard, bordering the road. PRINCE DEUKALION, seated on a rude stone bench, beside the fountain.]

PRINCE DEUKALION.

My limbs are weary, now the hoping heart
No more can lift their burden and its own.
The long, long strife is over; and the world,
Half driven and half persuaded to accept,
Seems languidly content. As from the gloom
Of sepulchres its gentler faith arose,
Austere of mien, the suffering features worn,
With lips that loved denial, closed on pain,
And eyes accustomed to the lift of prayer.
The suns of centuries have not wholly warmed
Those chilly pulses; scarce those funeral robes
Permit some colored broidery of joy;
And half the broken implements that fell
From conquered hands of Knowledge and of Art
Are still unwielded. From its first proud height
Humanity must bend; and so, neglecting these, —

Defenceless through its ignorance renewed, —
One pair of hands has grasped the common right,
And one intelligence the thought of all!

Are he and she, who now approach this shrine,
Other than when the conquering demigods,
Fair forms triumphant on high pedestals,
Sat where yon saint, head downwards on the cross,
Blends torture with distortion? What! Shall pain
Uplift and save, spilt blood and dreadful death
The fair, discrowned serenities of Gods
Make impotent? But I will hear once more
The subject faith, the helplessness, the fear.

[SHEPHERD *and* SHEPHERDESS *come foward and kneel before the shrine. Af-*
ter devotions made, they rise.]

SHEPHERD.

To her, Our Lady, Lily, Star of the Sea,
Five hundred have I told upon these beads;
To him, now, fifty: since he keeps the keys,
Somewhat he may expect. Save that our saints
Grow covetous of prayer as priests of pay,
And sins provoke in order to absolve,
Our faith were easy.

SHEPHERDESS.

She, if any, hears!
Her eyes are tender, and her virgin breast

Fed not more lovingly the Child of God,
Than mine feeds mine.

SHEPHERD.

        Ay, safe by chrism and cross
Is he: no demons near his cradle hide!
Fast goes with feast, the penance with the gift,
Like good and evil seasons: pay your dues
And make them debtors! 'T is a plain account
Heaven keeps with earth, unless the stewards lie.

SHEPHERDESS.

And, after her, how fair the martyr-youth
Who sees his coming crown, and will not heed
The arrow quivering in his golden side!
Lover to maids, to me a brother, son
To women age-despoiled, — could once his eyes
Droop downward, he would pity, love and save.

SHEPHERD.

Why should they make the Demons beautiful,
And give our shrines to holy ugliness?
Cecilia, sitting at her organ-keys,
And Barbara, queen-like with her large, calm eyes,
Should be my goddesses, dared I select:
One is too pure to guess men's easy sins,
The other wise to pardon. As we go,
Sing thou with me her mellow canticle!

                          [Exeunt, singing.

For the secret faith adored,
Thou wast sent, by spear and sword,
Out of Egypt to the Lord,
    Holy Barbara!
From the sun upon the sand
And the stars on either hand,
From the glory of the land
    Taken, Barbara!
By the victory over pain
In the tower where thou wast slain, —
By thy sacrifice and gain,
    Hear us, Barbara!

PRINCE DEUKALION.

In these new names extinguished miracles
Sweetly renew themselves : disparaged types,
Torn from the pagan world and set in ours,
Become again divine. But, stay! who comes
With brow unbound and visionary eyes,
And nervous hands that clutch as if they sought
The antique plectrum and the chorded shell?
No wayside orison arrests his feet,
Yet doth he pause ; a dream within his blood
Casts old divinity on yonder Muse,
And far Ægean echoes in his ears
Reach the forgotten sense.

THE YOUTH (*to himself*).

Be it sacrilege,
I must adore thee! Yea, with hands that touch
The wounds of him upon thy ruin throned,
Approach thee; none of all the hosts that save
So gaze serenely over strife and time,
Beholding Beauty, being beautiful!
I know not if I know thee; yet I know
What in my soul endeavors to thyself —
Seeks consecration! Vacant are thine eyes,
Cold thine insulted brow and mute thy lips,
Yet, Goddess, to thy menial place I bend,
And give thee honor!

[*He stoops and kisses the lips of the Muse.*

PRINCE DEUKALION.

She will give it back.

THE YOUTH (*after a pause*).

Who, then, art thou? No pulse in all my soul
Hast thou abashed; but, rather, force and flame
Of scarcely self-confessed ambition rise
As I behold thee: Somewhat of *her* face
Grows into broader majesty in thine,
But human, as in them that must endure.

PRINCE DEUKALION.

As *thou* must! Out of all that was I come,
Awaiting all that shall be; they that know,
Behold me ever.

THE YOUTH.

Let me know, behold!
Thou seem'st the shape of what I dare to dream.

PRINCE DEUKALION.

Do thou my work! Through hates and battles walk;
Eat bitter bread of strangers; lose thy land;
Give up thy gentle love, to find once more,
An angel guide, the lily in her hand;
Scourge brazen power, and hunt hypocrisy
To where it hides, the olden Hades lost,
In tortured circles of your later Hell;
Become a voice where terror sheathes itself
In music, Pity, a dove in whirlwinds tossed,
Pleads out of agony, and primal Love
And highest Wisdom set alike for thee
The gate of Dis, the mount of Paradise!

THE YOUTH.

Thou speak'st as mine own soul.

PRINCE DEUKALION.

The sight unsealed,
Without the courage, seeing, to advance,
Were but a curse; but thou shalt be a name
Which is eternal power, and from thy pangs,
As by fierce heat, the chains be fused apart,
Which now the tears of ages rust in vain.

[*Exeunt.*

SCENE II.

[*Grand hall of a palace.* MEDUSA, *seated on a throne of gold, a triple crown upon her head. Four Messengers standing near.*]

MEDUSA.

Say to the East, her gateway of return
Stands open, though the hinges creak with rust:
Whence came the light her darkness dare not bide.
The seven lamps of Dawn have followed us,
And grown to suns, above, beneath our feet,
On right hand and on left: the Day is ours.

[*Exit First Messenger.*

Say to the South, the savor of her gifts
Delights us as of old: the faint, thin breath
Of her ascetic watches, sprinkled blood
Of self-inflicted penance, speech grown hoarse

In solitude, and visions born of brains
Dishumanized, have reached us and refreshed!

[*Exit Second Messenger.*

Say to the West, we ask no more than she
Erewhile hath given, eager and whole assent;
So flashing back the surplus of her light
•As a strong sunset fires the unwilling East!

[*Exit Third Messenger.*

Say to the North, the firmest hand is love's!
Except in force there is no help: in faith
Abides no jealousy. We hear her threats
In patience, as the frowardness of will
That brooks no other, until taught by loss.
Let her find freedom, and, as heretofore,
Finding, be cheated! Dreams of passing days, —
Selected truth of ages, — which shall stand?
Foreseeing penitence, we pardon now!

[*Exit Fourth Messenger.*

(*Sola.*)

Not vainly did I bide my time : for Power,
A tree of cautious growth, shows stunted top
Until the meshes of its wandering roots
Have crept in secret to the choicest clay;
Then, shooting firm and spreading boughs abroad,
Resistance withers, rival force lacks room
Beneath its shade. Now, planted for all time,
Kings are my vassals, Knowledge bids me fix
Her bounds of liberty! By failure taught

To seem to lose for sake of later gain;
With small success, until the greater come,
Content; forgetful never of the end,
What hinders me to make my single will,
Sheathed in invulnerable divinity,
The world's one law?

[A pause; she listens.

"Growth is the law,—or death."
Who spake? Or was it some last echo blown
From ended struggles? Growth is mine to give!
Have I kept life for all that in the Past
Men clung to, fed the old, barbaric sense
With what it loves, and paved an easy way
Between two worlds to suit the halting crowd, —
And am not potent? 'T is the single life,
Proud of small gifts, defiant in brief power,
That mocks the broad authority of time.
Through vice or perfect virtue comes alike
Obedience; this because it questions not,
And that, from need of pardon. Having these,
Whatever third between them lies must soon
Bend, or be crushed: I rule, while I exist!

[*Enter* PRINCE DEUKALION *and* PYRRHA.]

PRINCE DEUKALION.

Hail, Cæsar's heiress!

MEDUSA.

                  Who art thou?   And why
Such greeting?

PRINCE DEUKALION.

I declare thee as thou art.
The phantom purple underneath thy stole
We see, who nursed thy young humility
That now is pride, intrusted thee with strength
To be the strength of men, and made thee free,
That each soul's freedom find its root in thine!
How much of duty in thy power survives?

MEDUSA.

I meet the needs and the desires of men.
What they expect, I give; the seed whereof,
Sown ignorantly on all the fields of the Past
By dead Religions, I have reaped for them.
The passion and delight of sacrifice;
The comfort out of self-abasement won;
The lofty symbols, flattering lower sense
Until the thing it touches seems divine;
The sweet continuance of miracle
That Faith implores, to feel its Lord renewed;
The sanctioned ear, where Guilt may find release
And surety of pardon, — these I give.

PRINCE DEUKALION.

These only? Treadest thou thy children down,
Lest they should grow beyond thee? Hast thou peace
For Man's illimitable questions and desires?

MEDUSA.

Yea! Through obedience, peace for each and all.

PRINCE DEUKALION.

Art thou, then, more than man? Through him thou
  art.

MEDUSA.

Thy speech offends: the race-begotten child
Is its own father's lord.

PRINCE DEUKALION.

                    Prove lordship, then! —
Display the rights bestowed, to balance them
Thou hast usurped! Man's reverence is thine:
Where bides thy reverence for Man? The Mind
That, seated in the universe of things,
Needs all its heritage, — the haughty doubt,
Twin-born with knowledge and of equal right,
Hast thou made free?

MEDUSA.

        I make not error free.

PRINCE DEUKALION.

Art thou, alone, establisher of truth ? —
Not also Man who made thee, the high God
Whose will permits thee ?

PYRRHA.

Tell me what keen charm
Thou usest, that my daughters turn to thee ?

MEDUSA.

Knowest thou thyself and askest ?

PYRRHA.

Yea, I know
The strength and weakness of an instinct foiled.
Sexless thyself, the secret of the sex
Is lightly caught by thee ; yet, be thou skilled
To weave ecstatic visions from hot blood,
And call heaven down to fill Love's emptiness,
There dwells a soul in woman past thy reach,
A need that spurns thy tinkling toys, a claim
Beyond thy lullabies of sense and sound,
And sweet division of Divinity
'Twixt us and Man !

MEDUSA.

Thine ? — or felt by all ?

PRINCE DEUKALION.

A myriad speak, though single be the voice!
We know thee, Gorgon! Though the tonsured head
Keep down thy sprouting snakes, the triple crown
Hide their renewal, yet thy stony glance
Betrays the ancient beauty, and its dread!
Why hast thou turned from that defenceless love
Which equalized all lives of men, to use
The mystery of terror? Why made stone
The souls that moved before thee, save in chains?
Many thy keys of power, for thou hast learned
To govern weakness: hast thou then forgot
That force and freedom live?

MEDUSA.

Perchance in dreams.

PRINCE DEUKALION (*advancing*).

Before thee, here, I stand! One Power decrees
Thy life and mine: subdue me if thou canst!
My children made thee, and shall overthrow!
Take strength from all the Past, on dreams presumed
Build empire, and exalt thyself, — *I* am,
I was, I shall be!

PYRRHA.

I no less!

MEDUSA (*sinking down upon her throne*).
Away!

CHORUS (*without*).
As a bed where the weary sleep,
As a chest where our gems we keep
Art thou, our Mother!

ANTI-CHORUS.

Spare us! we stand despoiled
Of the goods for which we toiled:
Thine is the hand that foiled;
There is none other.

CHORUS.

We bow, and our joys endure;
Assent, and the Future is sure;
Thy rule is highest.

ANTI-CHORUS.

We ask, as thy gifts decrease,
Knowledge that brings us peace,
Freedom, the soul's release, —
But thou deniest!

CHORUS.

Power and Mystery thine,
5

Surely art thou divine,
To reign forever!

ANTI-CHORUS.

Power, the child of Will,
Dares and defies thee still:
Even God shall not kill
Man's endeavor!

———•———

SCENE III.

[*Night. An open grassy glade, between groves of ancient oak and ilex trees, in a deep mountain valley. The full orb of the moon hanging low in the west.*]

PYRRHA (*sola*).

In this pure shadow every rocky scar
Is healed: there is no lightest lisp of leaf:
The waters, only, never lose their song,
But in their swift, dissolving syllables
Some soft response to mine immortal hope
Endeavors for a voice. Most, unto me,
The time is holy: wherefore not to him?
Not weariness of baffled toil alone,
Nor late revenges of subjected sense,
Dare shape his dreams. Our primal task the same,
Our purpose one, our equal bliss through each
Ordained, at need I summon him to me:

From toil, uniting while it seems to part;
From visions of thyself, renewed
To quicken men's discouraged fortitude;
By the twin right of one inseparate heart,
    Which speaking, other voice is dumb, —
        I bid thee come!
If thee I most may comfort, or me thou,
    What need to question now?
    We take, even as we give,
Nor, save in our unreckoned bounties, live!
Deukalion-Pyrrha, all myself in thee
        Compels thee unto me!

[*A pause.* PRINCE DEUKALION *appears.*]

One moment, ere thou speakest, let me gaze!
Though some bright rosier flush of waxing life
Forsake thy features, marbled by the moon,
Thine eyes remain, and out of shadow send
A happy splendor: am I fair to thee?

PRINCE DEUKALION.

Fair and so near! Ah, Love, couldst thou be mine,
Save first myself were mine!

PYRRHA.

                Then I were less
Than thou believest; but my heart forgives
The over-fondness· of complete desire.

I venture further, dream diviner end:
Each lost in each, one body as one soul;
Endless renewals of surprise and bliss;
A twofold touch of life, all knowledge grown
A double power through interchanging sense,
As light should warm at will, and heat illume;
Two mingling tones to every passion's voice;
Twin-rays from eyes, as shines from sky and stream
The single star — but that were Deity!
We will not look beyond the task designed.
Guide thou thy sons as I my daughters; teach
Respondent honor to heroic blood
That wastes itself in self-forgetting toil;
Give rank and right, and exercise of rule;
With lighter weapons of one temper arm
The softer strength, and in one squadron set,
To fight the world's long battle!

PRINCE DEUKALION.

                              Force is kind,
That once oppressed, and honors fade unworn.

PYRRHA.

A favor on a·helm, — a tourney's crown!
Cross-hilted swords, in dying unction held,
Crimsoning scarf or glove! In lordly bower,
Or under oriel, lute and lay espoused
In adoration that purveys to sense,

While lowly virtue is a jest of fools!
What *she* bestows, the Head whom all obey,
Degrades while it exalts, a s'anctity
Conferred on bondage! Why, methinks, the world
Is but a monstrous wizard, weaving spells,
And chanting, under breath, some siren-song,
That none escape!

PRINCE DEUKALION.

Pyrrha, I read thy mind;
But till the snakes upon Medusa's head
Shall turn to tresses, and be loosed to dry
Man's bruisèd feet, or Man himself shall rise
And crush them under his avenging heel,
We must endure to wait.

PYRRHA.

How long?

PRINCE DEUKALION.

Not long!
There are who know me, whose allegiance went
In flame aloft, to fall in thunder back.
The winds of earth are wafting to and fro
The ashes of great lives, that seem, to Her,
The Gorgon, dust; yet are unquenchable,
Immortal fiery seeds of voice and act,
Her hate increases when it would destroy.

So Arnold lives, and Abelard: so he,
The youth I chose, shall with consuming song
Burn his broad way through ages! Thou and I
Before one onset walk; and thou shalt change
The old dependence into loftier aid.

PYRRHA.

Exact one space, where we may stand alone,
And unassailed!

PRINCE DEUKALION.

　　　　　Pyrrha! when proudest thou,
Dearest and most desired! Full-limbed and fair,
Such perfect beauty in thy lifted head
It cannot be defiant, such clear truth
In thy large eyes, such glory as a mist
Around thee —

　　　　　　　　　　　　[*Seizing her hands.*

　　　　Let it be a dream — no more!
Thy hands, a dream, and, ere the vision end,
Once let me know the lips that shall be mine!

　　[*Thunder. The Shadow of* PROMETHEUS *rises.*]

PROMETHEUS.

Not yet!
Slow-paced is Fate:
All crowns come late.
Couldst thou forget?

PRINCE DEUKALION.

Since my proud task began,
Nor more nor less than Man
Am I, or may become.

PROMETHEUS.

Haste is not speed,
And Passion mars the deed;
And Love's too-early pæan soon is dumb.

PYRRHA.

But in thy scheme lie burning
Keen sparks of yearning, —
The hope that dies not,
The voice that lies not,
The dream, more bright at each returning!
Within thy reed of stolen fire
Came down the Gods' desire,
Not their chill calm of changeless being.

PROMETHEUS.

Whence they, foreseeing
Far overthrow,
Through what of them in you was planted,
Made me your Expiator!

PRINCE DEUKALION.

The One we know,
God, Father and Creator,
Himself to Man his nature granted!

PROMETHEUS.

He standeth sure.
A spark of Him in all, —
The form of faith that dies,
The tenets that surprise, —
Though falling as ye fall,
He rises as ye rise:
He will endure!

[*The moon sets : a faint light in the eastern sky.*

PYRRHA.

Father, thou readest in my heart
What I implore, ere thou depart!

PROMETHEUS.

Though a sudden darkness fills
All the hollows of these hills,
White and large, against the gray,
Sparkles Phosphor's chilly ray;
And the mountain-brows are wan
In the weakness of the dawn.
But the little streak that lies

At the bottom of the skies,
As the remnant-wine in cup,
Fast shall fill and mantle up,
And, where yellow coldly grows,
Burn to gold and flush to rose.
Look, and hearken, if there be
Message in the morn for thee!

[PROMETHEUS *disappears.*

PYRRHA.

Wait, my Deukalion! hand in hand,
With quiet pulses, beating bliss in each,
And the immortal faith that asks no speech,
   Again beside me stand!
   Even now the glowing tide
Throws its first foam of fiery cloud, and wide
   The heads of mountain-peaks
Feel day's fresh blood upon their pallid cheeks:
Already sings aloft the awakened lark:
   Whether she come or fail, the Hour
   Brings consolation and swift power,
And I am strangely happy,— Hark! Oh, hark!

EOS (*unseen*).

Mother of them to be,
Who wast first designed in the Past
To be fulfilled at the last,
   Why calleth thy soul to me?

PYRRHA.

For the beauty my daughters wear
Is made to itself a snare!

EOS.

Beauty alike shall soften and save,
        Till Force shall feel,
        As the galley's keel
Is lifted and sped by the lovely wave!
Under the law that holds me afar,
And Fate's immutable bar,
By the secret of something all divine,
The heart in my bosom answers thine!

PYRRHA.

Not yet uncurtain thine eyes!
    I ask no more.

EOS.

The slow swift ages wait in the skies;
The ghosts are eager on Heaven's floor.
What Darkness sowed the Light shall reap,
    And Evil that reviled,
Impregnate in her drunken sleep,
    Shall bear a purer child!

                                    [*A pause.*

PYRRHA.

The roses fade, the music melts away.

PRINCE DEUKALION.

It is another day!

———◆———

SCENE IV.

[*The Roman Capitol.* MEDUSA, *throned on a platform, in front of an ancient church, in the walls of which are seen columns of a Doric temple. An immense multitude gathered together.*]

MEDUSA.

Who all possesses, dares be generous;
And here, where fell the guardian god of Rome,
Touched by a babe's soft hand, — where Cæsar's crown,
Descending, stopped when Tibur's Sibyl spake,
Foreseeing mine, — shall go indulgence forth!
No bounty equals that which Power bestows
That might withhold: the senses must not starve,
Lest the soul clamor. Out of what I hoard,
Prepared for me, the harvest of the Past,
Some ears may well be scattered.
                                    Who demands?

[*Two step forth : the* POET, *in a red mantle, his head crowned with laurel ;
the* PAINTER, *bearing tablet and pencils.*]

THE POET.

Faithful to all thou seemest, I have sung;
Hate is my portion, yet I sing no less.
Love for Love's sake instructed first my tongue,
That Truth so speak, and Justice so redress.
I am a voice, and cannot more be still
Than some high tree that takes the whirlwind's stress
Upon the summit of a lonely hill.
Be thou a wooing breeze, my song is fair ;
Be thou a storm, it pierces far and shrill,
And grows the spirit of the starless air :
Such voices were, and such must ever be,
Omnipotent as love, unforced as prayer,
And poured round Life as round its isles the sea!

THE PAINTER.

Faithful to all thou seemest, I have made
Thy glories visible, in beauty, grace,
Pain, death, and triumph! I have set thy saints,
In tints exalting life above itself,
And aureoled faces caught from ecstasy,
For endless worship. Vassal unto thee
Therein, the separate service now outruns
My vassalage ; for beauteous Art compels
Her Beauty's freedom !

MEDUSA (*aside*).
                     Freedom? still the moon
These children cry for.
                     Yet for thee there pleads
No crownless Muse, of them that haunt the ways
Of men, and think they live: thine never lived!
But of the others whoso linger still,
Long out of service, living on men's alms,
Decoying pity through their old respect
And fallen honor, — let them now appear!

[*Enter* THE MUSES.]

So much of dignity in ruin lives?
Save that some faces smile, and some are calm
With certainty of ancient place renewed,
Ye were defiant: but your pride is fair!
It suits me well to find dependent now
Such haught existences: as I grant leave,
Ye may endure: in them who served the old,
The newer faith rewards like loyalty.
First of the triple triads those advance,
Who nearest, lightest-natured, cheerfullest,
Were loved of men, and made the moment speed!

EUTERPE, THALIA AND TERPSICHORE.

In the woods and highlands
    We linger near;
By the shores and islands,
    When skies are clear.

Delight of existence,
　In the feet that fly,
Calls from the distance
　Our glad reply;
But the joys are sweeter
　That to all belong,
When the foot gives the metre,
　The heart the song!
No more you banish
　Than a cloud the sun:
We only vanish
　To be re-won!

MEDUSA.

Good service offers!—'t is the must of youth,
The hum, and surge, and sparkle of fresh blood,
That must have sway: be these my vintagers,
So mine the later wine! Yea, let the vats
Even over-foam, 't is sign of potent fire
Stored in the vessels when my seal is set,
And acrid strength of age. Without excess
Were less restraint: here may indulgence lie!
Go, altarless yet worshipped,—ye are free!

MELPOMENE, POLYHYMNIA AND ERATO.

When Music fails, and Joy is dumb
To men's exalted need, we come.
Our swords of sharper beauty cleave

The spells of senses that deceive,
And out of yearning, pain and power,
We call, and rule, one glorious hour!
Time cannot mar nor Conquest wrong
The swift, majestic march of Song,
Or Faith, in man's august desire,
Quench the least atom of her fire.
The Thought that strays, afar, alone,
We guide to speech and charm to tone:
The breathless Passions pause, to see
Their rage resolved to harmony;
The terror of their language wooed
To music, and to law subdued;
Till all things dread, fair, fugitive,
Touched by eternal Beauty, live!

MEDUSA.

These are suspect: whom shall they rule — or serve?

[*A pause.*

THE POET.

Me, if none other! Yonder multitude
Scarce knoweth what it loves, yet 'loves no less, —
Enjoys, forgets, discards and craves again,
Breathing high thoughts unconsciously as air:
Without them, stifled! Those are welcome now,
Who bring the sportive liberty of life
To the sad world's late holiday; but these,

Seldom as odors on the arid hills,
Still keep their fond surprises!

MEDUSA.

                              Under guard,
Then, let the Three go forth! They reach too high.
Who plucks on tip-toe at the dangling grape
Pulls down the vine: what's Passion but revolt?
What, save the music of illicit minds,
Is Poetry? Yet purposed deeds may sleep,
Lulled by the measure of their own wild dreams.
The accumulate store, saved from the wrecks of Time,
Frayed raiment, spangled thick with Pagan gems,
Is hoarded in my vaults; but at my will
Be spent the treasure!— easy luxury
To brains that else might coin, or claim, or steal.
These Three, of men surmised or coveted,
May walk the world henceforth; but, under guard!

CALLIOPE AND CLIO.

Daughters, whom Zeus and she,
Wide-browed Mnemosyne,
Gave to the sons of earth,
In wisdom, might and mirth
Divinely so to lead
That word is wed with deed;
And action, rhythmic grown,
Stands as in sculptured stone;

And noble speech commands
Service of swords and hands;
We wait, but do not ask
Continuance of our task!

MEDUSA.

Thou, of the keen, persuasive, perfect voice,
Thee I require!—despite the haughty flash
Of thine unshrinking eyes, I know the spell
That rules thee: wait, I'll feed thy tongue with fire!
Thou, too, whose stylus wanders restlessly
Across the empty tablets, at my feet
Sit down, and write me legends! I have store:
Pain, penitence, and power and miracle,
Glory, disaster, blessing,—by one soul
Informed, linking the ages in one scheme
Grander than all thy fables!
                              Who art *thou*,
The last, who speakest not? Thine eyes are set
Like one who sees not, thine attentive ear
Hearkens to something far away. Most fair
Wert thou, could Beauty, careless of delight,
Wear Wisdom's mask.—What Lamia lingers here?
                                          [*Aside.*

No supplication, nay, but pity shines
From those firm eyes: I cannot look them down!
Is it the coldness of the serpent blood
6

So chills me? Serpent?—one of us must writhe
When the end comes; but ages lie between.

URANIA.

The clear lamp, colorless,
Of high Truth I possess.
Hope, Will and Faith may spurn,
While fresh their torches burn,
What, kindling now afar,
Seems but a dying star:
Yet, wheeling as it must,
This little orb of dust
Not more the Law divine
Establishes, than mine.
Shall Faith permit me? Nay,
Thine standeth in my way!
The strong, unshaken mind
May shun me, but must find;
Devotion, bowed to thee,
Is upward blown to me,
Who over Change and Time
Stand single, strong, sublime!

MEDUSA (*rising suddenly*).

Seize the blasphemer! What!—from air she came,
To air returns? Or doth some shadow still
Glide past yon hoary columns?—She is gone!
Set double guards around our borders! Bar

With fire and steel her entrance ! Say, shall we
Hold parley with such immemorial hate,
Or, being Life to men, permit this Death
Her darts to scatter?
                    Take, new-wrought for you,
My children, chosen of the seed of Earth,
The timbrels and the flutes of joy; the pomp
Of color, music, marble, gems and gold;
The tender pardon of the whispered sin;
The symbols, fitting to the weary mind
An easy load, so keeping truth alive
In dusky mysteries; and, shadowing God's,
The universal watchfulness of Power!

> [*Exit* MEDUSA : *the multitude retires.*

THE POET.

(Solus, gazing down upon the ruins of the Forum.)

Urania ! — not thy face that earliest wooed me,
And from these ancient ashes called the fire !
Thy sister, even in marble sleep, subdued me
Unto free Song's untamable desire ;
And he, in whom I feel myself united
To deed and word and vision that inspire, —
Life's homeless Prince, alone in dreams invited, —
Is of thy race, and waits afar for thee.
What now thou art, Spirit so spurned and slighted,
I know not, nor can guess what thou shalt be :
But through the light of Day thine eyes are burning,
Thy feet are on the mountains and the sea;

The holy planets, going and returning,
Keep thy clear paths untangled in the sky:
Thy wisdom shall replace our hoodwinked yearning,
Thy living laws the mysteries that die!

———•———

SCENE V.

[A pass among the High Alps.]

EPIMETHEUS (*solus*).

Bright Earth! The echo of the fateful words:
" Rise, Brother!" scarce in twilight Hades dies,
And I behold thee! Bath of dazzling Day,
Take these spent limbs, revive the old Titan blood,
Sharp wine of mountain-ether! Are yon snows
Our Caucasus? — yon melting distances
The meads of Phasis, or, on Morning's side,
The Caspian and the far Chorasmian plain?
Here, now, the hoary, storm-tormented peaks
Stand silent: muffled thunders from below
Make brief disturbance: slopes of tender turf,
Untrampled by the steer, and flowers uncropped,
Smile a faint summer down the hollow dells,
And dark with lifeless water lies the lake.
There wheels a vulture, giving to the blue
The shade or sparkle of his slanted wings,
But seeking other quarry: not for me
Is torture, save the pang of growing sight,

And slow remembrance of the things that were.
The Past, that 'mid her ruins lay a-swooned,
In me recovers: pulse by pulse must I
Recall my life, and word by word my speech,
And age by age my knowledge!

[*Enter* URANIA.]

Also thou,
Whom, eminent in Babylon, I saw, —
Or wise in secrets of the Memphian stars,
Or hermitess on Samos, royal guest
In Academe, — endurest?

URANIA.

I endure.

EPIMETHEUS.

Where wast thou?

URANIA.

Waiting in the dust of earth
And the eternal splendor of the stars.

EPIMETHEUS.

Has thy day dawned?

URANIA.

Yea, ever is at dawn,
So men but lift their eyes!

EPIMETHEUS.

Where goest thou?

URANIA.

To them that seek me.

EPIMETHEUS.

Goddess, I return
To draw the forfeit forces of my youth
From dull, forgetful age: be thou my help!

URANIA.

Learn what to ask, I give: not mine to guess
The need of others. Epimetheus, thou,
A yearning shadow, must create thyself
And thine equality of final power.
Not yet thou knowest me; but, as I go,
Speak, soft, unsilenced Spirit of the Wind,
Speak, kindred Spirits of the Snow and Stream,
Declare my being!

[*She descends the northern side of the pass.*

EPIMETHEUS.

Spirits, I listen: speak!

SPIRIT OF THE WIND.

From the parched Numidian waste,
From the hills of hot Fezzàn,

I sprang with a boundless haste
  That only the stars outran;
Over mountain and Midland Sea
  That strove to tire or tame, —
Over Etna and Stromboli
  That pierced me with smoke and flame;
Till I laid, in the first desire
  That bended my pinions low,
The cheek of the sylph of fire
  On the breast of the gnome of snow!
For the powers of ruin, that meet
  In the vaults of space, must die
When the spirit that stays my feet
  Is lord of the tender sky!
I come, to wither and slay;
  I pause, to quicken and spare;
And the fate of the world I weigh
  In the trembling balance of air!

SPIRIT OF THE SNOW.

Homeless atoms, born in the sky,
Cling to the ledges bleak and high,
Fill the crevice and hide the scar,
And give the sunrise a rosy star! —
Gather and grow, till a shield is won
To blunt the spear of the angry sun;
Till from the heart of my chill repose
Power awakens and purpose grows, —

Out of my torpor the glacier goes!
Silent, certain, it crouches and crawls
Down the gorges in frozen falls,
And crystal turrets of azure walls,
Tearing the granite from crest and dome,
Hurling the torrent forth in foam!
Shepherding here my downy flock,
There I shatter the ribs of rock;
Stayed by a hand and slain by a breath,
There I am terror, and doom, and death!

SPIRIT OF THE STREAM.

Over the mosses and grasses
    The white cloud passes,
Silent and soft as a dream;
And the earth, in her shy embraces,
    Conceals the traces
Of the secret birth of the Stream:
Till my threads are braided and woven,
    And speed through the cloven
Channels, and gather, and sink,
And wind, and sparkle, and dally,
    With song in the valley,
And shout from the terrible brink!
Then the whirl of the wind divides me,
    And the rainbow hides me,
As I midway scatter in air;
And I bathe with endless showers

The feet of the flowers,
And the locks of the forest's hair :
Till proudly, with waters wedded,
    My strength is bedded
By meadow, and slope, and lea ;
And the lands at last deliver
    Their tribute river
To the universal Sea !

THE THREE SPIRITS (*as Echoes*).

Thou, to power and empire born,
Stay one arrow of the Morn ;
Pluck one feather from the wing
Of the wild Wind's wandering ;
Breathe to air the flakes that blow
From the chambers of the Snow ;
Hold one speck of drifting Force
From the measures of its course ;
Then of these hast thou the chain
Binding Man's immortal brain !

[*Enter* PRINCE DEUKALION *and* PYRRHA.]

PRINCE DEUKALION.

What faint, clear music of the elements
Makes all these mountains rhythmic, and this air ?
Thou hearest, Pyrrha ?

PYRRHA.

Not the same that fell
From fair Ionian stars, and found afar
Reverberant echoes on the mounts of Song;
But Earth awakens!   Hope I breathe, and power,
Losing my burden of remembered ill.

PRINCE DEUKALION.

New realms, yet not unknown, invite us.   See,
How, yonder, where the piny gorges fall
Northward, it spreads!—a land of tempered air,
Where Beauty's enemy, rough Toil, abides,
And all the joyous Muses bind their brows
With straightening fillets: never Daphne shakes
Her glossy head, or Pallas' hoary tree
Makes moonlight on the hills.   But Druid oaks,
Univied, stretch their stubborn arms abroad,
The firs bend black beneath their weight of snow,
The gray walls gloom, fire mocks the absent sun,
And Life, no more a lightsome gift of Earth,
Defends itself by battle: voices there
Call thee and me.

PYRRHA.

So but my daughters call,
They shall behold me!   Under placid brows
Of Nymph or Goddess, and the chaste cold breasts,

And beating through the snow of perfect limbs,
Is Woman! Beauty's soft inheritress,
Let her uplift her downcast lids, and see
Power abnegated, dignity unworn,
And equal freedom sheltering equal love.

PRINCE DEUKALION.

There lies Medusa's secret : with such bait
Long hath she fished; but thou shalt dis-immure
Her slaves, and give them their abolished sex!

[*Perceiving* EPIMETHEUS.

Here were a face — save that the kindled eye,
And April bourgeoning of sunny locks
Around the seamless forehead, might deceive —
I looked upon in Hades: is it thou ?

EPIMETHEUS.

Am I so young, then? What Prometheus mused
I know not yet. With sight indrawn he sat,
And seemed to listen, while our starless air
One weary hour hung dead,—then hoarsely spake:
"Rise, Brother!" and the thin, gray, crowding ghosts
Whirled on and would have risen; but I was here!

PRINCE DEUKALION.

What doest thou ?

EPIMETHEUS.

I listen.

PRINCE DEUKALION.
> Unto whom?

EPIMETHEUS.

The Wind, the Snow, the Stream. The mighty Muse
Bearing an orb, the star upon her brow,
Commanded speech of them, and passed beyond
To Thrace or Scythia.

PRINCE DEUKALION.
> She? — and thou? — Again,

O Pyrrha, let our severed hands unite!
Not mine the eternal secret of the Gods
To fathom, yet their purpose in my blood
Beats prophecy.
> Go, Epimetheus, sunward,

And seek thy childhood in the dust of ages!
Burrow in buried fanes: wash clean the altars,
And spell forgotten words on mouldering marble.
Perchance thy limbs shall fail, thy lids be weary,
And thou shalt sleep; fear not, I will awaken!
Thy brother's words fulfil: " Take one new comfort,
Still Epimetheus lives!" and now the morning
Shall not withhold the unseen eyes of Eos!

[*Exit* EPIMETHEUS.

PYRRHA (*as they descend the pass*).
Arching aisles of the pine, receive us ;
Dells of alder and willow, be fair !
Something of ancient beauty leave us,—
Gift for promise, and deed for prayer!

ECHOES.

In the shadows of the pine
Beauty waiteth, still divine:
She is thine!

PRINCE DEUKALION.

Will of manhood and blood of valor,
Leap as of old to the day at hand:
Free of doubt and of craven pallor,
Rise and ransom the captive land!

ECHOES.

In the forge and in the mine
Weapons for the battle shine:
They are thine!

[*Exeunt*

ACT III.

SCENE I.

[A valley among hills covered with forests of oak and beech. Below, in the distance, a richly cultivated plain, a city with Gothic towers, and a broad river, dotted with the sails of vessels.]

POET (*passing*).

EARTH, thou art lovely as any star,
With rest so near, desire so far!
Peace from the tree-tops on the hill
Sinks, and the blissful fields are still;
While tender longing, pure of pain,
Dwells in the blue of yonder plain;
And all things Fancy, faring free,
May clasp or covet, come from thee!
Something of mine is everywhere,
Trodden as earth or breathed as air;
Giving, with magic sure and warm,
Voice to silence and soul to form,
Calm to passion and speed to rest,
Borrowed or lent of mine own breast
By that swift spirit that mocks the eye,
As over thee the unfeatured sky,
Heaving its blue tides, endlessly, '

To planets that fail to lift the sea!
I am thy subject, yet thy king:
Give me thy speech, and let me sing!

[*Exit.*

GÆA.

Step to the music of the song I gave,
My Poet, homeward! Lovers, find in me
Your voiceless eloquence and balm of bliss,
That else were pain! Mine ancient life revives
With sweeter potency: I am a Soul
Responsive unto all that stirs in Man,
Transforming passion to a natural voice,
From airy murmurs of the fragrant weeds
To the hushed roar of pines, the tramp of waves,
And bellowing of the ocean-flooded throats
Of headland caverns! Wafts of odorous air,
The thousand-tinted veils of dawn and day,
The changeless Forms, that from the changing Hours
Take magic as a garment, stellar fire
Sprinkled from hollow space, and secret tides
Lifted by far, fraternal planets, — these
Have grown to speech, companionship and power.
Tired of the early mystery, my child
Hearkens, as one at entrance of a vale
Never explored, for echoes of his call;
And every lone, inviolate height returns
His fainter self, become a separate voice
In answer to his yearning! Not as dam,

With hungry mouth,—as goddess, with bowed heart
He wooes me; or as athlete, million-armed,
Summons my strength from immemorial sleep.
He comes, the truant of the ages,—comes,
The rash forgetter of his source; as lord
He comes,—lord, paramour and worshipper,
Tyrant in brain, yet supplicant in soul,
With fond compulsion and usurping love
To make me his!
    Still scorned are ye, fair Forms
I sheltered? Under yonder beechen shade
Hath human longing set ye? Hide my streams
Your beauty still, my mists your loosened hair?

  NYMPHS *(at a distance)*.

As the night-air pants;
As the wind-harp chants;
As the moonlight falls
Over foliage walls;
As gleams forerun
The smile of the sun
When clouds are parting,
Our beings are.
We are held afar
By a knowledge burning
In the heart of yearning;
For the necromancy
Of the fonder fancy

Breathes back into air
The Presences fair
It would fain restore:
We are Souls and Voices,
But Forms no more!

GÆA.

Ye highly live, more awful in the spell
Of unseen loveliness! No need to quit
Your dwellings, strike the dull sense into fear,
And win a shallow worship: Man's clear eye
Sees through the Hamadryad's bark, the veil
Of scudding Oread, hears the low-breathed laugh
Of Bassarid among the vine's thick leaves,
And spies a daintier Syrinx in the reed.
For him that loves, the downward-stooping moon
Still finds a Latmos: Enna's meadows yet
Bloom, as of old, to new Persephones;
And 'twixt the sea-foam and the sparkling air
Floats Aphrodite,—nobler far than first
These bright existences, and yours, withdrawn
To unattainable heights of half-belief,
Divine, where whole reflects the hue of Man.

NYMPHS.

In the upward pulse of the fountain;
On the sunny flanks of the mountain;
Where the bubble and slide of the rill

7

Is heard when the thickets are still;
Where the light, with a flickering motion,
From the last faint fringes of ocean
Is sprinkled on sand and shell;
In the ferns of the bowery dell,
And the gloom of the pine-wood dark,
And the dew-cloud that hides the lark,
The sense of Beauty shall feel us,
The touch of delight reveal us!

[*Exeunt.*

GÆA.

Fear not, sweet Spirits, what unflinching law,
Tracking creative secrets, Man may find
In my despotic atoms! Who denies
Confirms ye to the sense that bade him seek.
But thou, mine Eros, through whose ministry
Stole back the banished Beauty,—as, at first,
The harmless tear-like trickle of a stream
Through some Cyclopean dam, that softly wins
A vantage, till the whole collected lake
Sets its large lever to the trembling stones,
And freedom follows,—thou, who, well I know,
Hidest beneath this roof of summer leaves,
Or where the minty meadow-breath makes cool
Thine ardent brow,—appear, and speak again!

EROS.

I am not he whom Hermes overcame,
Nor always from my brother's grosser flame
    Held my pure torch afar:
New bows I span, new arrows fill my quiver.
Those twain, mine enemies, avoid me now,
Stung by the steady radiance of my brow,
    Nor, save in secret, mar
My lordship over them that I deliver.

The penance of the ages was in vain;
Old sweetness sprang from each invented pain,
    And Love increased by wrong,
And won supremacy by sharp denial.
Faith dungeoned him, till, pining for the day,
He stole the wings of Faith and soared away:
    So grew my nature strong
Through conquered violence, and pure through trial.

What though new strains enrich my airy lute,
The primal ecstasies are never mute;
    No throb of joy is missed,
Nor from the morn is any splendor taken.
But nuptials of the senses now repeat
The mystery of equal souls that meet, —
    That kiss when lips are kissed,
And each in each to sovran life awaken!

GÆA.

Not mine to guess thy riddles, — yet I see
Near manhood in thine adolescent limbs,
Proud lustre in thine eyes, as, through the joy
That still around thee sparkles, other joy
Made prophecy, but never of an end,
And mystic sweetness in thy budded lips.
Nathless, whenever my strong spouse, the sun,
Stoops nearer, sets his bosom unto mine
And stirs all fond, sad raptures of my frame, .
Then most I note thee, hurrying to and fro,
Sure in thy speed; or when he lingering leaves
My bed of long delight and summershine
With last caresses, thou on every hill
Dost walk in light, and breathest through the woods
Voluptuous odors of the yearning year !
Exalt thyself past limits of my law,
I feed thee still ! What soaring mist of mine,
Sun-gilded, but the iron frost of space
Shall seize ?   What odor reaches to the stars ?

EROS.

Nor the soul of the wandering odor, nor the light of
  the mist, is thine,
Who art rolled through day and darkness, at the will
  of a star divine ;
Who claim'st the arrows of beauty, alone from its quiver
  sped, —

Thou readest but half the riddle in the dust that else
  were dead!
Thy life is blown upon thee, as a seed from another
  land,
And the soil, and the dew and water, are the bounty of
  thy hand;
But the secrets of whence and whither are mine for my
  children's need :
I go with the flying blossom, as I came with the flying
  seed!

———⋅———

.

SCENE II.

[*A spacious square, at the extremity of a city. In front, a church : on one side
a cemetery, with an open gateway : on the other side a market.*]

PYRRHA (*looking towards the gateway*).

There, out of stubborn wrong and thwarted hope
And helpless ignorance, Earth has only gained
A heavier mould; and she must heap her dead —
As the slow ages on her bare emerge
Gathered the dust for grass, the deepening sod
For forests — ere our seeds of total life
Find rootage, and with undecaying green
Redeem this desolation!

PRINCE DEUKALION.

Yea, but eyes
That once behold, and souls that once believe,
Lend faith and vision as a lamp its flame!

PYRRHA.

Ay, Faith! that limits where it should enlarge, —
That sees one only color, where the sun
Brands ever three, nor suffers even them
To burn unblended!

PRINCE DEUKALION.

　　　　　'T is the curse of souls
That selfless aspiration looks above
To find joy, knowledge, beauty, waiting there,
Because abandoned here!

PYRRHA.

　　　　　So mine await:
They doubt me, not forbid me.

PRINCE DEUKALION.

　　　　　Doubt but feeds
The callow faith that has not tried its wings.
Be comforted!

PYRRHA.

Deukalion, is it time?

PRINCE DEUKALION.

How often, Pyrrha, have we watched the morn
Divinely flush — and fade! How often heard

Music, that, ere it bade us quite rejoice,
Died, echoless ! Yet Patience cannot be,
Like Love, eternal, save at times it grow
To swift and poignant consciousness of self ;
And something veiled from knowledge whispers now
Prometheus stirs in Hades !

PYRRHA.

Darest thou call ?

PRINCE DEUKALION.

I dare not. Epimetheus slowly clears
Back through the gloom and chaos of the Past
The path of his return. The widening sphere
His keener vision measures now for Man
Discrowns Tradition, shrinks the span of Time,
And throws the primal purpose of our fate
Once more upon us. Thus the Titan stands
Nearer than when the frosty fetters burned
His limbs on Caucasus !

PYRRHA.

And also she,
Pandora, freed from long disgrace of Time,
Since now her Hebrew shadow flings away
The fabled evil ! When the Past is purified,
We shall possess the Future.

PRINCE DEUKALION.

Yea, our source,
As from the bosom of a mountain mist,
Leaps out of Nature, innocent at last!
In our beginning Destiny divine
Set the accordant end; and this, obscure,
Makes that with monstrous intervention dark
To human souls. Already Earth is red
With ebbing life-blood of the wounded Faiths
That shriek, and turn their faces to the wall,
And shut their vision to the holier Heir,
Who, unproclaimed, awaits his lordship. Lo!
How he who governs these austerer lands
Withholds his gifts, betrays his promises,
Gives freedom for repentance, not for change,
Nor other answer than his own, to doubt!
Foe to Medusa, in his secret dreams
He wears her triple crown,—allows, perforce,
Urania, banished from her first abodes,
Chill hospitality, an exile's fare,—
No right of home! What will his welcome be,
When Epimetheus, hand in hand with her,
Tells the new story of the human Past?

[*Enter a Man and Woman.*]

PRINCE DEUKALION (*to the Man*).
Say, dost thou know me?

MAN.

At a distance, I
Have seen thee pass : I never heard thy name.

PRINCE DEUKALION.

I speak it not.

MAN.

Thou movest my desire
To know, yet, save the knowledge be allowed,
No less my fear : there's brightness on thy face,
As one who sees no pitfall in delight,
Nor snare in science, nor the burden bears
Of fallen nature.

PRINCE DEUKALION.

.   Whence is thine so dark?
Art thou in love with pain?

MAN.

I cannot help
Some joys of life, and guilty dreams of more :
But He who suffered for my sake forbids
That I rejoice too greatly.

PRINCE DEUKALION.

Wisdom, then,
Wilt thou accept?

MAN.

The wisdom of the world?
Nay: 'tis vain-glory.

WOMAN (*to Pyrrha*).

If indeed for me
Thou hast a message, as thine eyes declare,
Thou knowest my need.

PYRRHA.

I know thine ignorance.

WOMAN.

I would have knowledge, were the entrance free.

PYRRHA.

Want forces entrance, justifies itself,
As hunger crime! But learn what Beauty is,
And this, thy present weakness and reproach,
Becomes immortal power!

WOMAN.

When I behold
Thy face, I seem to own it.

PYRRHA.

Set thou, then,
Whatever visage unto thee I wear
Within the shrine of thy desires, thereon
To brood in longings born of motherhood,
That so thy daughters shall inherit it,
And I in them be nearer!

MAN (*to the Woman*).

Strange the words,
Their meaning doubtful: how shall thou and I,
Bearing Eternity's full weight alone, —
Ours all the debt, foreclosed if other coin
Save what our Faith supplies be given as due,
And poor in deeds that earn it, — how shall we
Accept such help? He wears the face of Power,
She that of Beauty; what if both mislead? ·

WOMAN.

Her spirit touches me, as doth the sun
A folded bud: if I become a flower,
The hue and fragrance locked within my life
Without my will are scattered.

MAN.

Come away!
[*They pass on.*

PYRRHA.

No more the shepherd and the shepherdess,
Our children! 'T is the wisdom of the school,
So grave in childish self-sufficiency,
That turns on Nature and disowns her bliss.
I know not what large hope awakens now:
Pandora, Titan-mother! rise and see
How speeds thy purpose!

PRINCE DEUKALION.

      Ere thou summon her,
Or he unsummoned rises, let us seek
The stately High-Priest who hath ruled so long
These broadening realms, advancing nobler fate
Even where he willed it not, the instrument·
Of that diviner mystery than his God!
The sky-cast shadow of a Hebrew Chief
Fades o'er his altars; and the aureoled Love
That later veiled the tyranny, reveals
A change in its intensest splendor wrought
Invisibly: if he hath eyes to bear,
His ear may hearken, when Prometheus calls.

SCENE III.

[*The interior of a spacious church. In the chancel a lofty altar, on the front panel whereof is carved a rayed triangle: on the top of the altar rests the Ark of the Covenant, above which towers a Cross.* CALCHAS, *High-Priest, stands upon a raised platform before the altar, clad in an ephod of gold, blue, purple and scarlet, with mitre, girdle and breast-plate of twelve stones, as described in Exodus xxxix.* PRINCE DEUKALION *and* PYRRHA *in the nave.*]

PYRRHA.

Still old the symbols!— and the spirit looks
Backward to whence they came.

PRINCE DEUKALION.

So should it look,
But free, across a conquered realm! The Past
Is Man's possession, not his mocking glimpse
Through loopholes of the jail where Reason pines.
It gives the Prophet vision, as a root
Declares the measure of the branch it feeds;
But here are teachers, who, to lead the blind,
Hoodwink themselves. What common eye can see
Past things as present, ancient miracle
To-day's dull fact, God's hand upon the man
It looks at? Over gulfs of ages these
First find their sanctity, as our dark orb
Drinks light from ether till it grows a star.

PYRRHA.

It is the heart that dares not look too near,
Nor yet too high.

PRINCE DEUKALION.

       The heart, that doubts the brain, —
Feeling, divorced from knowledge, — this it is
That neither loves us nor can be estranged;
That dimly plays with our conjectured will;
Obeys, mistrusts itself and grows ashamed, —
Then turns apostate!

PYRRHA.

       Nay, Deukalion, nay! —
That, born anew, retains the old desire;
That, kindled once, keeps memory of the flame;
That out of thwarted yearning, baffled peace,
And endless pangs of vain self-surgery,
Still floods all life with fond presentiment
Of thee and me!

       [*Sound of the organ.*

CHANT.

From this body of death deliver,
   This burden of woes!
We call, as they called where the river
   Of Babylon flows.

Like the wail of a captive nation
Is the sound of our lamentation.
From the pleasures that still delight us;
From the daily sins that smite us ;
From the difficult, vain repentance
And the dread of the coming sentence;
From the knowledge that gropes and stumbles;
From the pride of mind that humbles ;
From beauteous gifts that harden,
And bliss that implores not pardon;
From the high dreams that enslave us,
　　We beseech Thee, save us !

PRINCE DEUKALION.

Joy in Thy world divine,
And the body like to Thine ;
Pride in the mind that dares
To scale Thy starry stairs,
Rising, at each degree,
The least space nearer Thee ;
Strength to forget the ill,
So Thy good to fulfil ;
Freedom to seek and find
All that our dreams designed,
Driven by Thine own goads
Forth on a thousand roads;
Patience to wrest from Time
Something of Truth sublime,

Or of Beauty that shall live, —
We beseech Thee, give !

CALCHAS.

(Perceiving PRINCE DEUKALION *and* PYRRHA.*)*

I do mistrust these strangers. Since that she,
Medusa, thrust them out from all her realms,
What time she banished her of orb and star
I sheltered (threatening now with adder sting
For life revived), they wander to and fro —
Or others in their likeness, — and disturb
My settled sway. Freedom I gave, because
Free-will must choose me, — bade men seek the truth,
Because the truth conducts them back to me.
Urania, with her forward-peering eyes,
Saw not the vestments, which, to mark her mine,
I laid upon her shoulders : suddenly now,
Full-statured, with uplifted head she walks,
And drops her loosed phylacteries in the dust.
These, too ! — whate'er they purpose must be mine,
If good, since other good exists not : yet
They stir some quick perversity of heart
In man and woman, teach abolished needs,
And open gates I shut — but may not bar.
They come this way. I 'll question them.

PRINCE DEUKALION (*advancing*).
                                High-Priest,
Thou shouldst proclaim us, and thou know'st us not!

CALCHAS.
Much have I heard.

PRINCE DEUKALION.
                        What most ?

CALCHAS.
                        That ye do breed
Confusio 1.
PRINCE DEUKALION.
        Nay ! — but out of thine we build
The ruined harmony.

CALCHAS.
                        Then, enemies
Ye now declare yourselves, where I but deemed
Some seed of pride had sprouted o'er its fall.
What is 't ye do ?

PRINCE DEUKALION.
                        What thou hast never done,
Who hast one purpose where thy sons need all,
Who keep'st them puppets lest they grow to Gods !
8

CALCHAS.

I seek to save them.

PRINCE DEUKALION.

They will save themselves,
Not by one anchor which may drag them down,
But carried outward by all winds that blow
Into the shoreless deep! Give knowledge room,
Yea, room to doubt, and sharp denial's gust
That makes all things unstable! Tremble not
When stern Urania writes the words of Law:
Make once more Life the noble thing it was
When Gods were human, or the nobler thing
It shall be when The God becomes divine!

CALCHAS.

Blasphemer!

PRINCE DEUKALION.

Curse, if so it comfort thee.
Thy weapon, too, is terror; but when men
Cease to be cowards, idle Hell shall close.

PYRRHA.

Yield what thou canst: there still is time. Give up
Dead symbols of the perished ages: doff
The trappings of a haughty alien race
Whose speech was never thine: keep but the spark

Of pure white Truth which nor repels, forbids
Nor stings, but ever broadening warms the world!
Think what thy lips have promised, how thy hand
Rent suddenly our chains! Nearest thou art
Of them that sway the torpid souls of men:
So, then, be *all* where thou art but a part, —
Be all, teach all, grant all, and make thyself
Eternal!

CALCHAS.

Am I not so, now?

PRINCE DEUKALION.

Not yet,
Save in the taste of that thou offerest, —
Repentance.

PYRRHA.

And thou mightst be, in thy love.

CALCHAS.

Repentance? Love? What words are these you speak?
One wins the other: I announce them both,
And all beatitude that follows them.
Beyond the curse inherited by flesh,
Beyond this cloudy valley, where as rain
Fall human tears, and sighs of vain desires
Make an incessant gust, I know the way
To refuge, and the one permitted bliss
Of living souls.

PRINCE DEUKALION.

Let me behold that bliss!
I have the right of entrance: fear thou not!
The phantom key thy hand yet seems to clutch
Lend me a moment; or, canst thou not yield,
Then stand aside!—O Father, is it time?

PROMETHEUS (*rises*).

What matters, whether soon or late?
Thine is the burden, thine the fate.
Long hast thou waited, not too long,
For patience is the test of wrong;
And thee the slow years may allow
Some right of deeper vision now.
The trial art thou strong to bide,
Explore thy way!—there is no guide.

[*Disappears.*

PRINCE DEUKALION.

(*Seizing the horns of the Ark upon the altar.*)

I know what holy mysteries were thine
In the old days: but what art thou become?
Yield up thy spells to one who saw thee pass
Through the dusk halls where Amun-Ra was lord,
Or Nile-borne on thy barque of flowers! What lore
Of wandering souls — of life beyond the end —
Is thine to give us?

[*A pause*

Nothing more than this? —
Gray emptiness of space, with here and there
A flying shadow, whether man or fiend
The eye detects not: something vast of form,
Yet Hebrew-featured, stirred to mighty wrath
By hostile Gods, defending, as it seems,
A throne secure, — uncertain of His will,
And undecided if His sons shall live.
They, too, poor ghosts! must hover on the verge
Betwixt two worlds: they reach no firmer soil
Of airy substance, yet which may upbear
Thin feet of spirits, but in endless whirl
Drift through the shapeless void. I 'll look no more.

[He lays his hand upon the Cross.

Symbol of Fire, the oldest, holiest!
Forget thy speech on Asia's hoary hills,
Dip thy pure arms in blood of sacrifice,
And tell me what thou heraldest!

CALCHAS.

Avaunt!

PYRRHA.

There is less profanation in his act
Than in thy prayers. Be silent, — wait the end!

[PRINCE DEUKALION'S eyes close: he slowly sinks down and lies,
leaning against the altar.

SCENE IV.

THE VISION OF PRINCE DEUKALION.

As out of mist an unknown island grows,
It swam in space, surrounded with repose.
" Behold," an airy whisper said, " the sphere
Through hope existing, as yon pit through fear;
For what men pray for — while they pray — shall last,
Since Faith creates her Future as her Past."
No light of sun, or moon, or any star
Touched the white battlements that gleamed afar,
Or painted with strong ray the pastures wide
Between slow stream and easy mountain-side,
But over all such cold and general glow
As moonlight spreads upon a land of snow,
Yet fairer, shone; and myriads wandered there,
Giving no stir to that unbreathing air,
White as the meadow-blossoms, and as still,
And white as clouds on each unshadowed hill.
A city vast, that bore an earthly name,
With thousand pinnacles of frost and flame
Stood in the midst; and twelvefold flashed unrolled
The pavements of her avenues of gold,
Where harps and voices one high strain did pour
Of " Holy, holy, holy !" evermore.
And out the, centre, from the burnished glare,
A golden stairway sloped athwart the air,

And faded upward, where a Phantom shone
That changed in form to them that gazed thereon.
These, side by side, and wing caressing wing,
Rested like wild doves on their wandering,
Innumerable : and o'er them seraphim
Winnowed rich plumes to make the glory dim,
And children's faces, kissed with sweeter light,
Circled in swarms around a Throne of white.
Shapes of no sex, too beautiful for man,
Too cold for woman, spread the rosy van
And slanted, shining, far amid the space.
Some pleasure came on each uplifted face
To see those messengers, — some rapid awe,
When that high Form, with hidden brow, they saw, —
But else their eyes were weary, and the fold
Of each white mantle slept upon the gold.
Dead seemed their hands, save when the harps they smote
And made accord of one perpetual note.
The entrance of a living spirit there
Gave a quick motion to the torpid air,
Startled the light with shadow, and breathed out
Keen earthly odors ; yet of dread or doubt
Among the myriad myriads was no sign.
A listless wonder woke in souls supine,
But made no speech, for consciousness was numb,
Save to the awful voice of what must come,
As on dead continents the live sea's roar :
    " Forevermore !   Forevermore ! "

PRINCE DEUKALION.

Angels, a moment stay
Your heavenly errands, and betray
What nature, beautiful and dim,
As in some twilight dream of power
Is born for one bright hour,
Ye have received from Him !
Shorn of all kin are ye,
Companionless, unwed
With primal mortals, loveless, passion-free,
Not living, neither dead !
Declare me this :
Is it your only bliss
To sail, soft-shining, with your wings outspread ?
To cheat the ecstasy ye cannot share,
With apparitions fair ?
To give each holy dream
Its warranty supreme,
The palm to promise, and the lily bear ?

ANGELS.

We cannot know :
We are the feather, His the breath to blow.
Though human yearning mould
Our passive being, we are cold.
Pity, to eyes that mourn ;
Passion, to hearts that burn ;

Reward, to lives that dare ;
Salvation, unto prayer, —
What face men look for, such we wear !
Unborn, we have no destiny,
Nor other being than to be;
Nor service, but to soar
'Twixt One Adored and many that adore.
What should we further tell ?
Thou hast no message : so farewell !

PRINCE DEUKALION.

But ye, Transfigured, whose denial
Endured the life-long trial, —
Pure souls, whose only human terror
Made Thought an ambushed error, —
Who now possess, secure from losing,
The bliss of your own choosing,
Speak, are there needs ye here have sighed for,
More than on earth ye died for ?

SPIRITS.

Is it permitted ?

PRINCE DEUKALION.

I am here.

SPIRITS.

We tremble, yet we must not fear.
The bright temptation of thy brow
We once resisted, conquers now;
But thought unused and voice unheard
Deny us the consenting word.

PRINCE DEUKALION.

Look on me, and it shall be given!

SPIRITS.

O joy! O pain!
As leaves from autumn boughs are driven,
At last, at last,
Thy will hath torn us from our Past,
And half we live again!
Yea, here is glory, here is bliss,
Arms that sustain us, lips that kiss,
And rest, and peace, and pain's reward
In that pure light which seems the Lord;
But — bliss without endeavor,
And lips that cannot part;
And rest that sleeps forever
In each immortal heart;
And light whose splendor hideth
The Face we burn to see —
What is it that divideth
Eternity and thee?

PRINCE DEUKALION.

I am eternal, even as ye.
But your concealed, undying woe
Is this : ye have not sought to know.

SPIRITS.

We did obey.

PRINCE DEUKALION.

But whom, ye may not say.
Have ye beheld Him?

SPIRITS.

Nay.

PRINCE DEUKALION.

Once more upon Him call :
Uplift awakened eyes!
Though falling as ye fall,
He rises as ye rise.

SPIRITS.

His Will in dreams we saw,
And left unlearned His guiding law;
We forced our lives to crave,
Through bondage, what His freedom gave ;
Till, having fondly wrought,
We own the Paradise we sought, —

. Self-bound, and over-blessed
With endless weariness of rest!

One multitudinous sigh was breathed along
The golden avenues, and shook the song:
But far aloft they heard a trumpet blown,
And keen white splendor gathered round the Throne.
Then slowly up the ether-darkened blue
The meads and hills and battlements withdrew,
Till all the sphere became a silvery moon,
With ever-lessening disk, and star-like soon,
And faded out: but in the hollow space
All suns and planets kept their ancient place.

SCENE V.

[A wide plain, uninhabited, dotted with ancient mounds. EPIMETHEUS, seated on a fallen pillar, at the doorway of a half-exhumed palace, with a broken tablet in his hand.]

EPIMETHEUS.

It is the speech I heard but yesterday,
When all this buried pomp stood bright in air,
Terrace on terrace, till the topmost seemed
Fit for the feet of some descending God,
While bannered masts and galleries of sound
Hailed him, invisible; and whispered words
To consecrated ears, these tablets bore;

And the wide shadow of this power was thrown
O'er half the world. What said Prometheus then,
When, groping first on fields of unblown mist,
I sought to hold the ever-vanishing forms
With stable vision? — " 'T is the Future's gift,
To know the Past!"
                     Yet I had mused, not slept,
Through weary ages : 't was alone their dust
That made me seem so hoary. Action, now,
And waxing knowledge, destiny fulfilled,
Restore the ardors of Titanic youth.
Though lost the primal struggle, lost the joy
That even defeat to high defiance yields,
I am at last a Power, and challenge Powers, —
A truth, and thus a terror! In my, veins
Burns eager blood; I know my brow is fair,
My voice hath music, and the ears of men
Perforce must hearken, as I tell the tale
Of ever older and of mightier Pasts,
Lost tongues and sacred secrets, stolen faiths,
Perverted symbols, and the favor shed —
One tribe usurped — upon the Chosen All!
                [*Enter* URANIA.]

URANIA.

What doest thou here?

EPIMETHEUS.

              I triumph !

URANIA.

Wherefore now,
More than erewhile?

EPIMETHEUS.

I have remembered that
Forgotten, when I saw nor understood;
And now remembered since I know.

URANIA.

(*Taking up a handful of dust.*)

And I
Have found in this the secret of all worlds.
Thy Past? I know no Past! Thou dream'st of time,—
It is not, was not! Nothing is, save Law.
Thy feet are on my paths: not heeding them
I guided thee, yet in so much of power
As may be given thee, more of freedom lies
For them that follow me and cannot turn.

EPIMETHEUS.

Proud wast thou ever.

URANIA.

Proud, because assailed,
As who, with full hands bearing gifts, is spurned.

EPIMETHEUS.

Yet pause! I am no longer slack of thought:
I know thy being. Though I give return
Of needed help, the will which sent me forth
Hath still some ancient empire over thee.

URANIA.

Yea, thou art wakened! Why should I conceal
From thee, thus proud, associate soon with him,
Thy brother, whose large vision moves with mine,
The ultimate barrier where I needs must pause?
But thou, and every Titan yoked with thee,
And every track that other knowledge treads,
And all the visions unto Faith allowed,
Reach not so far: what matter if I halt,
Not impotent, where no disturbance comes
To vex me, resting but a little while?
Push back that point where thou rememberest not
Through countless æons, still thou find'st my trail!
Grasp thou the seeds of life in sun and star,
And sink then, fainting, where I stand and smile!
'T is not subjection, but a limit, rules:
My work is baffled since I could not give
The primal impulse.

EPIMETHEUS.

                      Neither thou, nor he,
Prometheus!

URANIA.

          Cease! — thy words renew the chill
That seizes me at each new victory.
The cry of old affections shakes my hand;
The gush of human heart's-blood comes to dim
My crystal eyesight; and a something lost,
Because unsought, perchance unsearchable, —
Unknown, because unknowable to sense, —
Assails my right.

EPIMETHEUS.

          There is no enmity
Where neither can be lord: do thou thy task,
I mine, and each eternal Force its own!

———◆———

SCENE VI.

[*The shore of the open ocean : morning.*]

PRINCE DEUKALION.

Thou lookest eastward, past the gem-like round,
The sky of opal and the sea of pearl:
I surely misinterpret not thy hope,
Or is 't thy longing?

PYRRHA.

Say, my haughty faith,
That will not pray for what it must expect.
Once have I called on Eos, but I call
No more : the silver echo of her words
Repeats itself within me, as their vows
To happy lovers. Thus it was she spake :
  " Faith, when none believe,
  Truth, when all deceive,
  Freedom, when force restrains,
  Courage to sunder chains,
  Pride, when good is shame,
  Love, when love is blame, —
These shall call me in stars and flame ! "
Thence call I not; but, yonder, as I gaze,
The twin stars, visible no more to sense,
Glimmer, the phantoms of her eyes; the red,
Now fading, is her cheek's immortal flush,
And the loose golden opulence of her hair
These clouds untangle.

PRINCE DEUKALION.

                    Here her face revealed
Would doubly promise, as the mirroring wave
Doubled her loveliness. The conquering Gods
Made too much haste to seize a mountain-throne :
This were their seat; but old Poseidon took

The realm that should be Jove's, where, set between
The unknown silence and the noise of earth,
Are two pure elements, pavement and dome.
Here glimpse upon the soul imagined shores ;
Here Fancy out of changeful air may build
Her far-off palaces ; yet what of truth,
Accepted fate or world-defying will
Exists, confirms as well its being, here.
Time is the billow, Destiny the shore.

PYRRHA.

Deukalion ! Seest thou naught?

PRINCE DEUKALION.

                  I see the gray
Of waves that first shall darken to the sun ;
The distance, where no separating line
Cuts the soft web of sky-inwoven sea ;
And all the dipping rondure of the world
Beneath it, where the mighty Day looks down,
Or sadly lingers for the word and deed
Undone, unspoken !

PYRRHA.

             Ah ! as out of air
It suddenly grew, I see a glorious barque
With bellied canvas of the morning cloud,
The cordage of translucent vapor spun,

The hull a curve of sea-foam, foamlessly
Borne onward, silent, with unruffled prow
Approaching us! Two forms direct her speed,
And either's arm is on the other's neck,
And locks of gray and gold are mixed above
Their equal brows. Thou hast not called them?

PRINCE DEUKALION.

Nay,
And yet, beholding not, I know the twain.
Oh, come ye hither from the unmeasured Deep,
And not from Hades? Come ye with the morn,
Unsummoned, though the morning's goddess fail?
Come ye, at last, whose birth reversed your fates,
United, one in knowledge, one in power?
Father, and thou, alike a father, hail!

[PROMETHEUS *and* EPIMETHEUS *appear.*]

PROMETHEUS.

What language hath, to-day, the sea,
To chill, inspire or menace thee?
What eager hope or spleen forlorn
Blew on thee through the gates of morn? —
Or were thy power and purpose dumb
To speak our coming, ere we come?

PYRRHA.

Not in dejection did we brood,
Hearkening the many voices of the sea.
But for the scattered spirits free
Which lure, yet mock, the captive multitude;
And for these last, who yet
Can neither learn new things, nor old forget;
And to fulfil thy plan
That woman shall be woman, man be man,
We pondered, here apart,
One wisdom for the brain and heart!

PRINCE DEUKALION.

Not in dejection, no!—while every Force,
Once idle, formless, unto Man becomes
A god to labor and a child to guide;
While Space, obstructing human will no more,
Makes Time a tenfold ally; while the draught
Of knowledge, once a costly cup, invites
Free as the wayside brook to whoso thirsts,
And aspiration, trying lonely wings,
Escapes the ancient arrow! These are gains
We cannot lose; but what new justice comes
With them, to right Earth's everlasting wrong?
The weariness of work that never sees
Its consequence; chances of joy denied
To noble natures, prodigal for mean;

Helpless inheritance of want and crime;
The simplest duties never owned untaught,
The highest marred by holy ignorance;
Crowned Self, that with his impudent hollow words
Is noisiest, and Vanity that deems
His home the universe, his day all time!

PROMETHEUS.

These are, and they shall be;
Nor less, though thine impatience fret.
Man is a child upon thy knee,
And earth his cradle yet.
Unto thy voice his quickening ears
Open a little space,
Till, taught by dreams of countless years,
His eyes shall know thy face.

PYRRHA.

I stand as one that after darkness feels
The twilight: all the air is promise-flushed,
Yet strangely chill, and though the sense delight
In sweet deliverance, something in the blood
Cries for the sun. Ye know, who set my work,
It is no selfish passion. Shorn are they,
And by the fondest fate, of action's crown,
My daughters, — so, denied their part
In old divinity and balanced right
Of man's prone worship, losing thence

Some honor Time is ignorant to restore,
They need their equal half of all there is,
Uniting, not dividing, Life. Who twains
What once was one, makes both more grandly one;
Or thou and I, Deukalion, could not be!

PROMETHEUS.

Now should Pandora speak!
Withdrawn the demigoddess sits,
And silent, yet there flits
A flush across her cheek,
A soft light o'er her eye,
And half her proud lips smile:
Unto thy hope, the while,
Be this enough reply!

PRINCE DEUKALION (*to* EPIMETHEUS).

What bear'st thou from thine East?

EPIMETHEUS.

                              The living Past
That from its grave my former being caught,
And left me youth.

PROMETHEUS.

                  Which, backward sent .
To Man's dim childhood, where thy memory dies,
Foresees with me.

EPIMETHEUS.

And active even as thou!
I bring dread knowledge: change and overthrow,
Despair of creeds, and shaking of the shrines,
And fruitless building till the Builder come,
Are in my hands. The Gods of races I
Unseat, as Time or Tyranny of old
Unseated them, by one subversive lore
Of equal truth revealed to them that seek,
None self-elected as depositors,
But His eternal Covenant with Life
For all, forever!

PRINCE DEUKALION.

Who shall teach that lore?

PROMETHEUS.

Its whisper now sets every wind of earth
Vibrating: hearken, here!—the subtle sea
Hath learned it from the happier stars, and bears
The message to his loneliest isles; the buds
Expand it in their blossoms; helpless souls
Discover it and rejoice, forebode and flee.
Truth gathers being as the fire in air,
Until, surcharged, it drops a blazing bolt
And speaks in thunder.

PRINCE DEUKALION.

Who shall hurl those thrones,
Untenanted, beside all wrecks of Power,
And dwell above them, that mankind may rise?

PROMETHEUS.

He is unknown.

ECHOES.

Unknown! — yet known.

PROMETHEUS.

He is alone.

ECHOES.

Alone! — yet with His Own.

ACT IV.

SCENE I.

[A vast flowery meadow : the sea, cities and mountains in the distance.]

AGATHON (*a child*).

(*Solus.*)

SOULS know their errands, — yet must live,
Ere speaking, all the truth they give.
Sad must their brooding childhood be
Who teach the old captivity,
And ah ! how sad, perplexed and strange
Is theirs who see, but cannot change ;
How dark who build not, yet destroy, —
But mine, at last, but mine is joy !

No herald star announced my birth ;
Men know not that I tread the earth ;
I fashion not the doves of clay
That, when I bid them, soar away ;
Nor twine the rose, in sportive need
To make prophetic temples bleed ;
Nor look, from eyes of early woe,
The agony I shall not know !
O Purest, Holiest ! — not thy path
'Twixt tortured love and ancient wrath

Is mine to follow: none again
Wins thy beatitude of pain:
But all the glory of the Day,
All beauty near or far away,
All bliss of life that, born within,
Makes quick forgetfulness of sin,
Attend me, and through me express
The meaning of their loveliness.

Yonder, the weary, longing race
Conjecture my maturer face,
Nor dream the child's — when they behold
Beneath its locks of sunburnt gold —
That only says: " My life is sweet;
The crisp, cool grasses love my feet;
The lulling air my body takes
To slumber, and the wave awakes;
And pleasure comes from soil and flower,
And out of lightning falls a power,
And from the breath of ancient trees
The vigor that enriches ease,
And from the mountain-haunted skies
The will that ruins, save it rise!"
Be the white wings of Duty furled
To-day, and let me own the world! —
The azure flag-flower basks in heat,
Yet cools, below, her plashy feet;
The footsteps of the breezes pass

In shadow-ripples down the grass,
And glimmers, where the pool is thin,
The slide of many a silver fin.
Beam on my bosom, warmth divine,
Until its pulsing currents shine
Like yonder river's! — pour the flame
Of supple life through all my frame,
Till consciousness of beauty there
Gives me the glory I should wear!
My limbs shall float, my motions be
Each a new change of ecstasy,
Nor shall I breathe except to know
What savors the swift airs bestow,
While pure, as when its beats began,
The heart to music builds the man!

I know I AM, — that simplest bliss
The millions of my brothers miss.
I know the fortune to be born,
Even to the meanest wretch they scorn;
What mingled seeds of life are sown
Broadcast, as by a hand unknown,
(A Demon's or a child-god's way
To scatter fates in wilful play!) —
What need of suffering precedes
All deeper wisdom, nobler deeds;
And how man's soul may only rise
By something stern that purifies.

But here I gather, ere my hour
Shall call, the fresh, untainted power
Of Nature, half our mother yet,
And angry when her sons forget.
Far as the living ether bends
My being through her own extends;
Frèe as a bird's to sink and soar
O'er meadow, mountain, sea and shore;
One with the happy lives that breed
Their like in spawn, and egg, and seed;
One with the careless motes that stray
To gather gold for dying day,
And with the dainty sorcery
Of odors blown far out to sea,
That say to mariners on the wing:
The unseen earth is blossoming!
But farther, finer, airier yet
A soul may spin its mystic net,
And, with unconscious heart-beat sped
Vibrating on each gossamer thread,
Declare itself and all it gives,
Though, speaking not, it simply lives!

SCENE II.

[*The interior of a spacious church, as in Act III., Scene III. Noon : the win-dows are open, and the nave is filled with sunshine.* URANIA, *slowly pacing down the main aisle.*]

URANIA.

An added step, and these groined arches fall!
The mine beneath the fortress of my foe
Is dug, the fuse is laid, and only fails
One spark of fire, but such as must be stolen
Elsewhere than from mine atoms. How, save I,
Myself, create, shall I creation solve?
Exalted thus, and throned on rigid Law,
That bids a million universes whirl
In the inconceivable Immensity, —
Earth but a mote, and all humanity
Its faint result, — shall I admit desire
As cause, not sequence, fondest dreams as fact,
And vast inflation of the vapory Self
Beyond all spheres of sense? With my large scheme
This last breathes interference : unto me
Myself suffices : no fond paramour
Shall woo me for my beauty, save as truth
Makes beautiful, or knowledge stands for love.
Men's minds grow wider : my serener light
Probes the dark closets of the mystic Past,
And many a bat-like phantom, blinded, shrieks

For the last time, and dies: yet — one more step,
The final one, awaits me.

AGATHON.

(*Appearing from behind the altar.*)
Yea, and that
Thou canst not take.

URANIA.

What hinders me? — speak on!

AGATHON.

Then thou wert God!

URANIA.

The Cause? the first impelling Force?
The Ages yet. may make me so.

AGATHON.

And Man,
Who, knowing thee, is everything thou art,
Shall find himself created by his will,
And all his faith in one advancing life
Through fairer spheres is thine in being his!
Almighty Love, lord of intelligence,
Anointed Prophet of Eternity,
Lives, even as thou.

URANIA.

And dies, when thwarted law
Prohibits.

AGATHON.

Nay! — not dies, howe'er obscured
Or mutilate, — not dies, in that dense dark
Where thou art impotent, but is the ray
That guides men to thy feet and far beyond!

URANIA.

I know thou canst not be mine enemy;
Yet why, to flatter life, wilt thou repeat
The unproven solace?

AGATHON.

Proven by its need! —
By fates so large no fortune can fulfil;
By wrong no earthly justice can atone;
By promises of love that keep love pure;
And all rich instincts, powerless of aim,
Save chance, and time, and aspiration wed
To freer forces, follow! By the trust
Of the chilled Good that at life's very end
Puts forth a root, and feels its blossom sure!
Yea, by thy law! — since every being holds
Its final purpose in the primal cell,
And here the radiant destiny o'erflows

Its visible bounds, enlarges what it took
From sources past discovery, and predicts
No end, or, if an, end, the end of all!

URANIA.

I know this dialect, so many strive
To make it mine, or bend my tongue thereto.
Let there be truce while perfect knowledge waits!
Here cometh one whom I must serve, — and thou,
If thou wouldst live.

[*Enter* PRINCE DEUKALION.]

AGATHON.

My father!

PRINCE DEUKALION.

Have I, then,
In some exalted trance begotten thee? —
Ah, not from her who only should have nursed
Thy babyhood, — *our* race is yet to come.
Thou hast my features, and from heart and lip,
As thus I hold them swiftly unto mine,
Flow sweetness; and the light in thy young eyes
Is as a hope within me.

AGATHON.

And my work
Shall bring me nearer, since, if thou wert not,

I could not be! My hands are tender yet,
My feet too lightly borne, my soul alive
With too much joy: I feel, but cannot teach,
And wander, guided by a shaft of light
That shall illumine knowledge as I need.
Whither, I question not: I only know
It touches thee, or thy far phantasm set
Where fades from earth the beam, so linking us
In one design. The first art thou to know,
The first to love me, — and wouldst first command!

PRINCE DEUKALION.

I have awaited thee a thousand years.

AGATHON.

I waited for my time.

PRINCE DEUKALION.

Our blood thou hast:
So might Prometheus speak. But wilt thou, here
Where gray Tradition hews each separate stone,
And vainly gropes decrepit Faith to clutch
The outflown Deity, transform the shrine
Where He, so starved by penance, comes no more,
But elsewhere stays until His feast be spread?
Some natural odor of the happy earth
Breaks in with thee: the arches clasp above
With leafy lightness of the summer boughs:

10

The oriel drops rose-leaves, and the font,
Bubbling and brightening with an inward life,
Spins up in silver, tinkling as it falls.
What hast thou done?

AGATHON.

At first I took away
The High-Priest's mitre, long since threadbare grown,
Eaten by moths, dust-soiled and shapeless. He,
As one forgetful, sought, then seemed to wear,
And with a customed hand to set aright, —
Then missed, forgot again. His ephod, next,
Of fine-twined linen, scarlet, blue and gold,
The girdle and the breast-plate of the tribes,
I hid from further use, — a sorer loss,
Awhile in his bewildered looks betrayed
And halting speech; but now he scarce recalls
That such things were nor could be otherwise.

PRINCE DEUKALION.

What next?

AGATHON.

What still remains; and — now — I do!

[AGATHON *removes the tablet with the rayed triangle, takes the Ark of the Covenant from the top of the altar, and conceals them.*

PRINCE DEUKALION.

The Cross endures.

AGATHON.

             Till some diviner type
Of man that loves and gives himself for men,
Shall plant his emblem!

PRINCE DEUKALION.

             O'er it, set a star,—
Beneath, a sphere!

AGATHON.

             Man must invent his own;
And this, that his far memory antedates, —
Descended with him from the world's cold roof,
Where, past the Indian peaks, on high Pamere
His race was cradled, — from a single death
Took sanctity forever! Whether mine
Be star or sphere, it is not mine to choose;
For I must pass ere I am known of men,
Who seeing, hearing, loving me, perchance,
Behold the brother, not the future god!

                          [Exeunt.

SCENE III.

[The court of a grand, dusky temple, with beams as of cedar-wood, supported by gilded pillars. At the further end, a veil, through which sculptured cherubim are indistinctly seen. On each side are thrones, overlaid with gold, set in the interspaces of the colonnades.]

PROMETHEUS (*solus*).

The sportive genii of illusive form,
Of hidden color and divided ray,
Have built me this, the ampler counterfeit
Of thine, O Solomon! that lifted up
Moriah into flashing pinnacles,
And spoiled umbrageous Lebanon to roof
Its courts with cedar! Less than air is mine,
The ghost of thy barbaric fane, yet meet
To hold the ghosts that deem themselves alive,
As in a truce of spirit, when the Dead
Float gray and moth-like through their wonted rooms,
Are shaped in dusky nooks to living eyes,
And send the hollow semblance of a voice
To living ears, — the law that parts them both
Being all inviolate. Such unconscious truce
I now proclaim, as ever in large minds
Holds back the narrower passion, and decides.
The conflicts of the earth must sometimes pause,
Breathless: some hour of weariness must come
When each fierce Power inspects its battered mail,

The old blade reforges, or picks out a new,
While measuring with a dim and desperate eye
The limbs of Man's new champion. Agathon !
Thy soul is yet outside the fiery lists :
The trumpet hath not called thee : as a child
Thou waitest, but the wisdom of a child
Must first be spoken. From their seats of rule
I summon them whom thou shalt meet, — and thee !

> King of the glorious reign,
> To whom thy glory slain
> Returned for all men's gain, —
> Queen of the triple crown,
> Whose haughty eyes look down
> From heights of old renown, —
> Priest, that wast sent to be
> Deliverer, but mak'st free
> Only who follow thee, —
> Muse, that hast grown so high
> Through the unmeasured sky,
> Man knows thee but 'to die, —
> Come, or the phantom send,
> Commissioned to defend !

[*The forms — or phantasms — of* BUDDHA, MEDUSA, CALCHAS *and* URANIA *appear, and seat themselves upon opposite thrones.* AGATHON *enters and advances to the centre of the temple-court.*]

BUDDHA (*dreamily*).

Across my bliss of Self absorbed in All,
And only conscious as a speck of dust
Is of its Earth, there creeps such faintest thrill
As to the lotus-bulb or rose's root
Strikes downward from the sweetness of the flower, —
The sign that somewhere in the outlived world
A God-selected soul is ripe to ask
A question that compels reply. I wake,
As one that, hammock-cradled under palms
Beside a tropic river, drinks the breath
Of clove and cinnamon orchards, seaward blown,
And through the half-transparence of his lids
Sees from the golden-gray of afternoon
The sunset's amber flush, but never fade.
Art thou, fair Boy, the questioner? Thine eyes
Demand Life's secret: learn thou to renounce,
And grow, renouncing, sure of Deity!

AGATHON.

But I *accept*, — even all this conscious life
Gives in its fullest measure, — gladness, health,
Clean appetite, and wholeness of my claim
To knowledge, beauty, aspiration, power!
Joy follows action, here; and action bliss,

Hereafter.! While, God-lulled, thy children sleep,
Mine, God-aroused, shall wake to wander on
Through spheres thy slumbrous essence never dreamed.
Thy highest is my lowest!

MEDUSA.

So speaks Youth,
That fans a calenture in spirits light :
With such I deal not, but its answering chill.
What refuge hast thou for the weary soul
That says : " My feet are bleeding ; carry me,
And I will serve thee " ?   Fretful is the race,
And breaks its playthings like a petted child.
But, looking backward o'er the heritage
That makes me holy, thee nor like of thee
Do I perceive : whose warrant sent thee here?
If Man's half-lost and consecrated Past
Thou canst restorē, be welcome! — otherwise
New heresy and hate are born of thee.
Lo! my commands are heard ; I do not change ;
Nay, though the headlong world transform itself
And speak strange tongues, in me all truth begins,
In me is finished!

AGATHON.

(*Advancing to the foot of* MEDUSA'S *throne.*)

Wake, O Sorceress,
Caught fast in thine own toils!   Wash thy filmed eyes

And look around thee! Why, what things are these?
Terror is gone from men, and Ignorance
Girds his weak loins, and all usurping hands
Of mediation grope for lost appeals,
Since that dread simulacrum thou didst frame
From breath of prayer, and altar-smoke, and gold,
Falls, and is God no more! A thousand years
Have passed since thou, in plenitude of power,
Didst set thy house in order, smile well-pleased,
And softly say: "Now may I sleep awhile!"
Yea, though the night-lamp bearing, thou hast walked
The chambers to and fro, 't was still in sleep,
And drowsed from changes of the sunlit life
Outside, till all thy Past slid down, and drifts
Where now it harms not: waken, if thou canst!

MEDUSA (*starting*).

What place is this? Who else is throned, where I
Alone am crowned?

AGATHON.

Let them declare!

CALCHAS.
(*Lifting his hand mechanically to his brow, then suddenly recollecting.*)
                                            No crown
He needs to wear whom happy followers love;
And unto these have I enlarged my gifts

Even as their souls discovered and desired.
I hold them not from seeking, but above
High wills and actions set the highest Good,
His gift, not mine. I war but with their pride
That, looking inward, finds too clear a light,
Too large a license, — looking upward, sees
A Deity too dim for mortal sense.

AGATHON.

Nay, Priest! — thou warrest with pure intelligence
That rays allwhither from its central flame,
And reaches God on Power's or Beauty's side,
As on Devotion's! Since thou wast content
With One whose human spite and jealousy,
Though veiled by later love, still shows the badge
Of clanship, men have passed thy visible fanes
To kneel in that invisible, whose wide walls
Surround all tribes, all upward-lifted lives,
All downward driven by ignorance and wrong.
Who reigns there sits above thy reach of soul:
Denial cannot 'scape Him, sacrilege stray
Beyond His pity, nor by any path
The seeking spirit miss!

URANIA.

              Save, indeed,
He be not else than universal Force,
And all His worship out of fibres born,

That, changing texture, change Him unto Man.
What eye hath known Him? What fine instrument
Hath found, as 't were a planet yet unseen,
His place among the balance of the stars?
But selfish fancy and insatiate love,
Chilled by almighty Law, demand to feel
A human heart-beat somewhere in the void,
And rescue their imagined essences,
Distinct and conscious, from eternal dust!

AGATHON.

That selfish fancy and insatiate love
Are thine, not knowing! Thou, without thy will,
Art the most glorious of the hosts that serve,
Proclaimer of the measureless scheme divine
That makes men tremble! In that universe
Thy lore hath found for His activity
Earth's petty creeds fall off as wintered leaves,
When April swells the bud of new. Men grow,
But not beyond their hearts, — possess, enjoy,
Yet, being dependent, ever must believe;
So with thy knowledge rises Him believed,
Shakes off as rags what once were holy names,
Treads under foot as crackling potsherds all
The symbols of old races, with one breath
Puffs into air defilement of their hates,
And stands alone, too awful to be named!
This is thy service.

PROMETHEUS.

Hast thou aught to ask?

AGATHON.

Verily, one seed is Truth's; but they who clip
The sprouting plant to hedge their close domains,
How should they know its grace of natural boughs
And blossoms bursting to the startled sun?
I ask them naught, fore-hearing their replies.

PROMETHEUS.

Forces that work, or dream;
Shadows that are, or seem;
Whether your spell sublime
Fades at the touch of Time,
Or from the ages ye
Take loftier destiny, —
I, of the primal date
As of the final fate,
Having compelled, release:
Depart, but not in peace!

[*The four figures disappear from the thrones.* PRINCE DEUKALION *and*
PYRRHA *enter the court of the temple.*]

PYRRHA.

O Son, thou last and sweetest hope for us,
Since men shall clasp thy truth in loving thee;

Where tarriest thou? The vault of golden air
Above thy meadows, knowing thee no more,
Is emptied of delight: the scattered homes,
Wherein thy face was precious, yearn and wait:
The cities and the highways of the earth
That know thee not, yet having seen thee, miss,
Are calling on thy name. Lo! we have sought,—
I and thy father,—sorrowing, for thee.

AGATHON.

How is it that ye sought me? Wist ye not
That I must be about my Father's work?

SCENE IV.

[A vast, natural platform, thrust forward from the extremity of a mountain-chain. Upon it rise the unfinished walls of an edifice, only half the pillars of the façade being lifted into place; yet every block suggests the harmony of the complete design. Beyond it the height falls away into broad terraces, the first dotted with woods of oak and chestnut trees, those below with fig, olive and fields of vine, and finally sinking through orange groves to the palms and tamarinds of a great plain, divided by an inlet of the sea. PROMETHEUS, PANDORA, EPIMETHEUS, PRINCE DEUKALION and PYRRHA, on the marble steps leading to the portal.]

EPIMETHEUS.

We know ourselves.

PANDORA.

And love!

PROMETHEUS.

And work as one !
Divided by the Gods that portioned out
Parts of a single destiny to each, —
Divided by the darkness of the race
That sees in fragments, and by highest Will,
Forerunning Time so far with prophecy
· That even hope grows faint, and faith benumbed,
We stand united now !

PRINCE DEUKALION. ·

Thou in design,
We in fulfilment ; what is Time, henceforth ?
I know thee as the Titan who defied
Man's violent Gods, defending Man's own right,
And who, foreseeing triumph in the end,
Hast never made surrender. What I am
Is thine : I am thy form of victory,
First kindled with the stolen fire of heaven,
To make all wisdom, worship, power, faith, joy,
And beauty, one !

PANDORA.

And thou, my daughter pure,
My Pyrrha, fear not thou that this shall be,
Till Woman owns her equal half of life,
And, following some supernal instinct, finds
Her half of Godhead !

PYRRHA.

'T is not hers to doubt.

PROMETHEUS.

Once did we walk the earth unseen; but now
Men pause, and with a holy, sweet surmise
Behold us dimly : Pyrrha, Deukalion
Grow dear to many an eye that looks afar,
And vanish in the nearness. Brother, thou,
Whose mind reversed interprets all the Past
And so o'erlooks the Future, even as one
That scales a mount between two mighty vales, —
Who readest thus Faith's awful secrets, — thou
Art loved, and feared; but still our perfect day
Sleeps in the womb of an unrisen morn.

SHEPHERD.

(*On the terrace below, singing.*)

Where the arch of the rock is bended,
    Warm, and hid from the dew,
Slumber the sheep I tended,
    All the sweet night through.
Never a wolf affrights them
    Here, in the pasture's peace,
But the tender grass delights them,
    And the shadows cool their fleece.

I blow, as a downy feather,
The sleep on my eyelids laid,
And rise in the twilight weather,
Between the glow and the shade.
Too blest the hour has made me
For a speech the tongue may know,
But my happy flute shall aid me,
And speak to my love below!

PROMETHEUS.

These simple lives may own contentment now,
Unscared; for happiness it is that gives
Sweet savor unto worship. Men, as trees,
Take from the elements their separate food
And grow in concord with the season's will,—
Exempt not yet, unsheltered even as these
From fated evils, gnawing drouth at root,
Bough-shattering winds, the lightning's sudden spear,
And blackest ruin, when the forest's heart
Breaks in the vortex of the hurricane!
But each discerns his place, or, failing it,
Is gently guided, — honors,·in himself,
Symmetric health and noble appetites
He once insulted, —hears the choric chant,
Unenvious of the singer's golden throat,
And smiles when Genius speaks, as who should say:
" He knows me, and his mighty words are mine."

SHEPHERDESS.

(Singing in the valley.)

Uncover the embers!
With pine-cone and myrtle
My breath shall enkindle
   The sacred Fire!
Arise through the stillness
My shepherd's blue signal,
And bear to his mountain
   The valley's desire!
The olive-tree bendeth;
The grapes gather purple;
The garden in sunshine
   Is ripe to the core:
Then smile as thou sleepest,
His fruit and my blossom;
There's peace in the chamber,
   And song at the door!

PROMETHEUS.

The suns of milder centuries must gild
The snow of this young marble, ere one block
Shall cap the pediment, and flash to heaven
Its finished glory! Oft the laborers
Shall pause, grown weary of the vast design;
Oft shall old apathy return, old strife
Shake like a chained volcano 'neath the sea;

But ere men change it, every stone shall turn
To adamant, or rise by hands of air!
As from the evangels of all races God
Begins to be, the tongues of every race,
Quiring a strain that silences the stars,
Alone can worship Him! Not yet Earth hears
More than the quarriers' and the builders' hymns.

CHANT.

(From the opposite side.)

Fashion your chisels well
With the steel from a hero's hand,
  Who conquered, as he fell,
The freedom of a land!
  Forge, out of chains that break,
Hammers and clamps alone;
  And cut from a martyr's stake
A wand to mete the stone!
  But sing, as ye work, a strain
Of joy and of triumph pure,
  Of deeds that were not in vain,
And blessings that most endure, —
  As a hope and a happier grace
Round the lives of duty poured;
  And the stone shall find its place
In the Temple of the Lord!

11

PRINCE DEUKALION.

Quick, fiery thrills, which only are not pangs
Because so warm and welcome, pierce my frame,
As were its airy substance suddenly
Clothed on with flesh; the ichor in my veins
Begins to redden with the pulse of blood,
And, from the recognition of the eyes
That now behold me, something I receive
Of Man's incarnate beauty. Thou, as well,
Confessest this bright change: across thy cheeks
A faintest wild-rose color comes and goes,
And, on thy proud lips, Pyrrha, sits a flame!
Oh, we are nearer!—not suffice me now
The touch of marble hands, reliance cold,
And Destiny's pale promises of love;
But, clasping thee as mortal passion clasps
Bosom to bosom, let my being thus
Assure itself, and thine!

PYRRHA.

Thine eyes compel;
Thy words are as a wind that bends me down,
And thou art beautiful as I to thee.
What holds me back? Is it that I perceive,
O Titan Mother, thy reproving face,
Immortal patience consecrates, and haste,

That pours too soon the beaker of the Gods,
Must ever trouble? Aid me with thy words!

PANDORA.

Take counsel of thy heart! The Gods themselves
Have seasons to rejoice; when happier eyes
Illume their ether, and unwonted lips
Meet, and their large refreshment falls on men.
Think what thou art, then follow thy desire!

[PYRRHA *muses a moment, then turns towards* PRINCE DEUKALION. *He
clasps her to his breast, and they kiss each other.*

———•———

SCENE V.

[*The Same.*]

SPIRITS OF DAWN.

Hark! has the Sun-god's Hour
Smitten her cymbals, dreaming him nigh?
We are called by a sound, and sped by a power,
    To break the sleep of the sky!
Æolian echoes blow
From the fourfold realms of the air,
And a torch, not ours, with a mightier glow
    Burns where the East is bare!
We hasten, we scatter the cloud:

We quench the beam of the great white star;
But the pæan is over-loud,
And the splendor comes from afar!
It flushes our halls of rest,
As the sun were a rose in hue,
And it paints the Earth, as she bares her breast
To the emptied urns of the dew!

[*Sound of Æolian harps; the face of* Eos *appears.*]

EOS.

Is this mine Earth?
The many-headlanded, the temple-crowned,
Which the great purple sea so whispered round,
When earlier Gods had birth?
Mine Earth, I loved so well,
Rejoiced in, as it welcomed me,
And fed with unexhausted hydromel,
While the young race was free!
I know its curving strands,
Its dimpling hollows, bosom-budding hills;
I scent large fragrance of the life that fills
The joined or parted lands.
Old hopes, and sweetest, burn again;
Old words are stammering on my tongue:
Was it your lips that kissed, Immortal Twain,
Or is Tithonus young?

PYRRHA.

As a gift unsought;
As a joy unbought;
As a fair hope fed   ,
From a hope that is dead;
As a diadem set
When the brows forget, —
Thou, the dearest,
Uncalled, appearest!

PRINCE DEUKALION.

Eyes of hope, and promise-laden
  Lips, that smile before they speak,
Are they thine, divinest Maiden,
  Blushing morning from thy cheek?
Unto prayer thy face denying,
Unto deed at last replying,
Linger near, and turn not from us
Present bliss and holier promise!

In the glory thou unfoldest,
  Tranced with music of thy tongue,
Young is all that once was oldest,
  Love and Faith and Will are young!
Stay with us! — thy smile assuages
Pangs bequeathed by weary ages,
And thine eyes are sweet forewarning
Of the world's eternal morning!

GÆA.

The blushes of thy cheeks descend on me,
Thy glance is glorious upon my mountains :
I breathe in ampler wind and prouder sea,
And beat, strong-pulsed, thro' mine unnumbered fountains.
Though filled with seeds of unimagined powers,
I cannot spare my beauty : now, from thee
Fresh silver stars the dewy-beaded flowers,
And rosy mists the fading forelands cover,
Until, far northward, thou dost pour
The rainbow's dust on every ice-built shore,
To make even sun-forgetting Death thy lover !

Am I not fair ? — yea, though thy face should bow
Thus near and fond, and find no child that knew thee :
But, having nursed Humanity as thou,
I feel what pure, prophetic rapture drew thee.
Stay thou with men ; take not away thy hope,
The endless answer to an endless vow :
Touch only, here, the risen Temple's cope,
And every glen and darksome lowland alley
Shall hail it as a herald ray,
And wait in happier patience for the day
When morning's mountain-gold shall flood the valley !

EOS.

Another must fulfil :
I am the promise, not the will.

Men dimly guess, through me,
 The distant glories that may be,
Renewed, as each grows pale
 In coming, through my roseate veil.
But, seeming o'erpowered
 When sunrise is strong,
Faith, Courage, Devotion,
 My being prolong!
I fade, for the coward;
 I flame, for the bold;
And noble emotion
 My face shall behold.
I grow from their yearning
 As they from my vision, —
No longer the Eos
 Of spaces Elysian,
But ever returning
 With promise sublime, —
First victor o'er Chaos,
 And last over Time!

PYRRHA.

To the gracious heart of Woman and the love that fondly
 bends,
Thou hast given the juster manhood that shelters it and
 defends:

For the Man's immortal ardor and the breadth of his
    soul's demand,
Thou hast set the woman beside him, and weaponed her
    equal hand;

As the palm by the palm in beauty, the female and the
    male,
When the south-winds mix their blossoms, and the date-
    sheaf cannot fail;
For one is the glory of either, since the primal Fate be-
    gan
To guide to a single Future Earth's double-natured Man!

CHORUS.

(From the valleys.)

Mother, thy work hath blessed us!
Honored, we wear thy cestus;
Honored, we lay it aside,
Crowned with the bliss of the bride;
Honored, we loose from eclipse,
Unto the sweetness of lips
Sweeter for innocent need,
Moons of the bosoms that feed!
Tender, for difference' sake,
Serve us man's haughtier powers;
Strength from his being we take,
But to restore it from ours!

PRINCE DEUKALION.

In the kiss of our lips that reddened
  With a perfect passion's dawn,
Met the bliss pure women yearn for,
And the noble truth men burn for,
When the youthful fancy is deadened,
  But the human heart beats on!

By the light of the dawn within them
  Their weakness my children see,
And Self and its greeds are broken
By the longing that dares be spoken,
And the warmth of the deeds that win them
  The courage to be free!

Still shy is the best endeavor
  That hath set its goal so high ;
But Good, when the heart betrays it,
And Love, by the lives that praise it,
Shall cradle the earth forever
  In the arms of a happier sky!

CHORUS.

(From the valleys.)

We hear thee and know thee, Father!
  As a flock the Shepherd leads,

We follow to thy pastures
  Of great and generous deeds.
Though suns to come may brand us
  And sudden frosts may blight;
And Crime, the prowling were-wolf,
  Steal on us in the night;
Though Self, that builds unwearied,
  May stain the purer will,
Or Apathy, slowly dying
  Of his own mortal chill;
Yet thou hast healing fountains
  Replenished from above,
In heart, brain, soul, renewing
  The triple strength of love!
Planted through all the ages
  Thy trees shall yield us food,
And goldening for our harvest
  Shall grow the natural Good!

PROMETHEUS.

Retrieve perverted destiny!
'T is this shall set your children free.
The forces of your race employ
To make sure heritage of joy;
Yet feed, with every earthly sense,
Its heavenly coincidence, —
That, as the garment of an hour;
This, as an everlasting power.

For Life, whose source not here began,
Must fill the utmost sphere of Man,
And, so expanding, lifted be
Along the line of God's decree,
To find in endless growth all good, —
In endless toil, beatitude.
Seek not to know Him; yet aspire
As atoms toward the central fire!
Not lord of race is He, afar, —
Of Man, or Earth, or any star,
But of the inconceivable All;
Whence nothing that there is can fall
Beyond Him, — but may nearer rise,
Slow-circling through eternal skies.
His larger life ye cannot miss,
In gladly, nobly using this.
Now, as a child in April hours
Clasps tight its handful of first flowers,
Homeward, to meet His purpose, go! —
These things are all ye need to know.

THE END.

www.ingramcontent.com/pod-product-compliance
Lightning Source LLC
Chambersburg PA
CBHW030900050726
47500CB00009B/547